RELATIVE STRANGERS

Recent Titles by Anne Worboys from Severn House

HOTEL GIRL

SEASONS OF THE SENSES

RELATIVE STRANGERS

Anne Worboys

This first world edition published in Great Britain 1997 by
SEVERN HOUSE PUBLISHERS LTD of
9–15 High Street, Sutton, Surrey SM1 1DF.
This title first published in the U.S.A. 1998 by
SEVERN HOUSE PUBLISHERS INC of
595 Madison Avenue, New York, N.Y. 10022.

British Library Cataloguing in Publication Data

Worboys, Anne

Relative strangers
1. Romantic suspense novels
I. Title
823.9'14 [F]

ISBN 0 7278 5296 5

Typeset by Palimpsest Book Production Limited,
Polmont, Stirlingshire, Scotland.
Printed and bound in Great Britain by
MPG Books Ltd, Bodmin, Cornwall.

Chapter One

'I have the most magnificent, wonderful, fantastic news for you.' That was what my friend Rosie had said over the telephone. 'Meet me at the Groucho and I'll spill all.'

So, she had won the lottery. Was to marry a lord. Had been promoted to editor of *Art and Galleries*, the magazine she worked for. All highly unlikely. Nonetheless, I hurried. I got off my bus at Charing Cross and walked up through Chinatown, past the red and gold lampposts, the windows full of dried fish and Peking duck, the fruit boxes set out on the pavement, oriental and exotic.

The Groucho is the watering hole of the Literary Establishment, where the people who count in that world like to be seen and the drinks cost the earth. Rosie was a part of all that. I hoped she was going to pay for my lunch. As physiotherapist to the disabled and otherwise unfortunate, by the time I treat myself to my weekly theatre seat – theatre being meat and drink to me as well as entertainment – pay my mortgage instalments and feed myself there isn't much left. My fees are well below the level at which one buys expensive lunches.

She was there at the bar, sipping a gin and tonic and beside her was a very good-looking man, slightly foreign in appearance with dark hair, though too big, I thought, to be either a Frenchman or an Italian. Tall like an Englishman. He was looking at me as I crossed the room in that way Italians have, frankly interested. Face. Breasts. Legs. Ah! I thought. That's some catch!

Rosie raised a hand in greeting and pointed to a glass standing on the counter. "That's yours," she said. The man merely continued to look and I realised, with a touch of disappointment, that he was not with her. That he just happened to be idly standing there, having a drink. I picked up the glass.

"Here's to you," I said.

"No." Her face was alight with excitement. "Here's to you." She shoved a shiny-paged magazine under my nose. "It's a trade paper," she said. "It gives lists of new publications and notes about authors and the books they are writing. It's on page eight." She thumbed through. "Now, don't die of shock." She folded the pages back to expose a paragraph she had marked in red and handed it to me. I took the magazine from her. Holding my gin in one hand and the magazine in the other, I began to read.

> 'One of the best kept secrets of the book world,' the article ran, 'is that the famous author Ben Tyrill is actually an Englishman called Andrew Hollis.'

Andrew Hollis, my father! For a moment I was quite unable to read on. My heart was thumping in my chest and my eyes refused to focus on the print. Everybody had heard of Ben Tyrill these days. He became known originally for his novels, but lately he had been turning out impressive art volumes with gilt print on the bindings, colour plates inside, and a lot of facts marshalled in superior prose.

"Read it!" Rosie was saying impatiently. "Read it."

I took a slug of my gin, blinked and made an effort to pull myself together.

> 'Hollis,' the article went on, 'has lived for many years in Italy, in a picturesque villa at Amalfi on the Gulf of Salerno. His publishers are anxiously awaiting his next book which will be on art and artists. Once a copyist and picture restorer, he is compiling a dossier of little known facts about the great paintings of the past. He claims he discovered methods of restoring and colour mixing while working as a student with the authorities in Florence, cleaning works of art damaged by the flood waters of 1961. He has held these secrets for thirty-five years. Now he's going public. Meantime he is playing hide-and-seek with the press. When a reporter tried to get an interview, Hollis was 'not at home' over a period of three weeks, during which time his familiar lean figure was seen emerging from the villa's grounds daily to swim from

the rocks below. His publishers say they are not worried. The book is scheduled for the spring, and Hollis has never missed a deadline.'

I had never known such excitement. It was spilling out of me. I wiped a tear away, glanced round to ensure I wasn't being watched and met the eyes of the good-looking man whom I had thought was with Rosie. He smiled. I glanced swiftly away.

"Clever old Rosie," said my friend, looking like a small, cute, smug Buddha. "What will you do now?"

I could not think. "It's fantastic!" I breathed.

"I agree."

"I can't tell you how grateful—"

She broke in to repeat, "What will you do?"

I said I did not know.

"Let's go and have some lunch."

She had a table booked already and had to order for both of us. My brain was in shock. Not working.

"Eat," she said, merry but a little impatient with me. "It's good food. Eat."

So I did. I don't remember that it tasted of anything. My taste buds must have been in shock too. "Listen," I said, "we'd better talk this out. If I write to him and don't get a reply, or a rebuff, that's the end."

"More or less." She watched me, intrigued and inquisitive.

"If I go to Italy and call, unannounced, at the villa . . ." My words faded while I thought it out. The fear in me favoured the latter. I did not want to risk a rebuff. Silence in the form of an unanswered letter was a rebuff.

Faced with his own daughter, on his own doorstep, could a man turn her away? Well, yes. He could. He had never met me. I couldn't be more of a stranger. It was said blood was thicker than water. What did that mean? Blood ties were supposed to be strong. If they were, why had he never visited me, or asked me to visit him? I glanced aside and again met the eyes of the foreign-looking man who had been standing by Rosie at the bar downstairs. He was lunching at a nearby table. Could I blame him for watching me? My face must have been a video of emotions. An author, I thought, studying his raw material.

I said, “I’m going to see Howard.” Howard is my stepfather. Goodness knows why I should rush off to tell him. Perhaps twenty-odd years of close proximity forms ties that are stronger than we realise. Or, I thought later, I had inherited a little of my mother’s naïvety. I suppose I felt I wanted, at this world-shaking moment, to tell someone, to be with someone, who had known my father.

Rosie said kindly, “Let me know.” She looked down at my plate on which lay the mess of broken fairy bread and paté that I had been toying with. “Hell, what a waste!”

“I’m sorry.” What else could I say?

My mother had been a warm, affectionate person whom my stepfather and I had equally adored, and who had kept us together in harmony. Her one fault, perhaps, had been her inability to make up her own mind. The three momentous decisions of her life were made by my own father, my stepfather, and Fate.

I had been there for Fate’s move. It had happened in January in a busy London street. Snow had been falling earlier in the afternoon. Now the temperature was dropping and it had begun to freeze. The road was very slippery. My stepfather took my mother’s arm.

“We will never get through if we don’t make a move,” he said. “Come on.”

“There is a zebra crossing only a hundred yards away,” I pointed out. It would have been so easy, so safe, to cross. But Howard was in a hurry. “Come on,” he said again.

“I am going down to the crossing,” I told them firmly.

My mother moved forward, then faltered. A car slid between us at the moment when she changed her mind and decided to take my advice. Between her and me. She fell under the wheels.

Howard and I parted after the funeral. Without real regret on either side, I believe. I had been part of the bargain when he’d married Mother. Now that she was no longer there, the bargain was null and void. My mother, who tended to see only that which she wanted to see, had never accepted the fact that Howard and I did not care for each other very much. Even in the making of her will, she followed this fantasy to its most illogical conclusion, leaving her money to him with the proviso that he look after me.

Perhaps she thought, naïvely, that by this method she would tie us together after she had gone.

In the event, he remarried within six months of my mother's death, as a man so often does when he has been happy in a partnership and is thrown off balance by the break. He chose a girl a little older than I.

"It's quite a responsibility, taking on a new family at my age," he said to me. "Carol wants children, and I have less than another twenty years of working life. I am sure you will understand when I say I will need every penny, now."

I understood. I had never known anything about my real father. Only that he and my mother had drifted apart and that I was the regrettable result of an impassioned and, as it turned out, futile effort to patch up the marriage.

"It was a long time ago," my mother said when I tried to talk to her about it. "One can't jump gaps like that. Yes, of course he knew about you. I mean, that you were going to be born. And that you were a girl, and the date. But by that time we had agreed that this patching-and-drifting was only making both of us unhappy, so we decided it would be better for you if we made a complete break, then and there. Howard had wanted to marry me long before I met your father. He was willing to take you and bring you up as his own."

"Why don't you try to trace your real father?" people asked after the accident.

I tried. I did not believe, as my mother did, that you cannot jump gaps of twenty years. And besides, I was lonely. But the London telephone directories, I knew, would yield no Andrew Hollis. I had looked the name up fairly regularly over the years, when new issues arrived. I wrote to all the people I knew in the provinces, but they reported no success. And there were those who kept reminding me, "He can't be any sort of father. He could have been in touch with you if he had wanted to. Isn't it better to let sleeping dogs lie?"

I telephoned Howard at his office. I didn't want to go to the house and meet Carol. That would have been embarrassing for both of us. He said he was tied up all afternoon.

"May I ask what it's about?" he asked.

I hadn't wanted to tell him over the telephone, but it seemed I had no choice. "I've found my father," I said, then repeated it in my excitement. "I've found my father."

"Oh yes," he said. "Well, if you could come in at three tomorrow. Would that suit you? Three? I could spare you half an hour."

I put the telephone down feeling numb and went out into the street. I walked down Shaftesbury Avenue and caught a bus at Piccadilly Circus that would take me back to the clinic. After a short time the numbness receded and euphoria returned. I was going to meet my father, at last. Blow Howard. Why had I not retorted, "Don't bother." I had nothing more to say to him. As I bought my ticket I thought, why did he offer me that appointment? He didn't want to see me. He must have a reason. And judging by his tone it wasn't a friendly reason. The excitement stayed but a niggle of worry had crept in.

The girls at the clinic were excited for me, and cooperative in juggling appointments so that I could see Howard at three the next day. "It might have occurred to him that you were working," one of them said, and that was true. I had thought his fixing that time was indicative of the fact that he wasn't concerned about me and my affairs. So why offer to see me? I hadn't suggested it.

"You'd better turn up," the girls said.

Yes, I had better. I couldn't very well call him again and ask why. I should have stopped to think before ringing him in the first place.

Howard is personnel manager at the headquarters of a big food chain. His office is in one of those tremendously tall buildings in a square behind St Paul's. I went up in the lift and his secretary showed me into his office. A stocky man, with a moustache and very blue eyes, he came from behind his large desk and shook my hand, then took a folded newspaper from a shelf.

"Sit down, Jane," he said, indicating a chair without arms on the opposite side of his desk. Probably his secretary's chair when she was taking dictation. I sat and he went back to his big, comfortable leather chair, leaned back, swung himself idly with his foot against the desk.

"You've seen this, of course," he said, holding up the paper and tapping it with the fingers of his free hand.

I frowned. This was not the magazine Rosie had shown me. "What do you mean?"

"The write-up," he said. "That's what you've come to talk about?"

"I saw it in a trade magazine," I said.

"Oh well, it's hit the tabloids now. They've listed the forgeries over the last twenty years, but they don't mention names."

I stared at him. Hypnotised. He looked back at me, blandly. "What do you mean?" I managed at last.

"Don't you know about the Raphael?"

"What Raphael?"

He reached across the desk and handed me the paper. "Read that," he said.

I took it. The article was headed, 'RAPHAEL FORGERY SUSPECTED.' And underneath: 'Art experts are being brought in to examine the Raphael that has been offered to a dealer in Amsterdam. Mr Rolo Seizerk, eminent Los Angeles art expert, has pronounced it to be a fake. He claims the original is held by a South American millionaire." Beneath another heading were listed various forgeries of the past.

"The first one they mention," said Howard, "was the one Andrew was involved in. Your mother never wanted you to know, but since it's come up again you are bound to hear, so you may as well hear from me. Raphael painted a series of Madonnas. This one has been discovered by someone in the Naples area. They're on to Andrew because that's where he lives."

"Why was I not told?"

"Told what?"

"That he lived in Italy." I thought of all those pointless searchings through English telephone directories.

"He didn't want to have anything to do with you," Howard said in that same bland voice, more cruel by far than any insult he might have delivered in anger.

I pretended to be unaffected, though the humiliation and disappointment were crowding in on me. It was like having the weight of the universe on my shoulders. I was beyond tears.

Inside my head was a cry of pain. I looked out through the big, oblong window, over the towers and rooftops of London to green trees that could be as far away as Dulwich. Such a view! I clung in my mind to its beauty while crushing the stirring emotions. I kept my eyes dry because I was a grown woman who did not need a father.

This man who was gazing at me across the desk, I recognised, had to punish me for all those years he had to live with me in order to have my mother. I saw the poison swirling in those blue eyes. I knew he was indulging in long-awaited revenge. My mother had been heavily pregnant when they married. How he must have hated that. How he must have loved my mother to do it. She had told me they hurried the divorce through so that I might have my stepfather's name. Everyone naturally assumed I was Howard's child. I was about fourteen when he told me I was not. After that, with my agreement, he changed my surname.

"Andrew and his partner owned a gallery in Bond Street," my stepfather said. "About the time you were born there was a great scandal. They were accused of selling forged old masters. The partner committed suicide, and the case against Andrew was not proved. But he had to close the gallery. He left the country."

I somehow knew, then, what had happened. That the story I had of the break-up of my parents' marriage was not entirely true. "Was that why Mother left him?" I asked. "Because she knew—" I corrected myself, "—thought he was forging old masters?"

Howard took his time about replying. "Margaret was a very conscientious mother," he said. "Can you imagine that she would want her daughter brought up by such a man?"

"The case wasn't proved," I said, carefully keeping the indignation out of my voice.

He shrugged, indicating, I thought, that my mother had made her own judgment. "Andrew never came back to England," he said, damning him and at the same time revealing his own guilt, for don't the guilty always shift the blame? I thought it was possible Andrew hadn't come back to England because he couldn't bear to see Howard with his wife and child.

"Did the partner who committed suicide leave a confession?" I asked.

"I don't believe so."

I took it he meant no. Of course he would have known if there was a confession. It would have been in the papers. Everyone would have known.

Perhaps in order to shield himself from the indignation in my eyes he rose, went to his briefcase which was leaning against the wall, and lifted it onto the desk. "I brought some letters in this morning. I found them among your mother's possessions after her death. I meant to give them to you if you turned up again. This might be a propitious moment." He slipped the clasp.

I knew then why he had not seen me yesterday.

"I'm surprised you didn't give them to me before," I couldn't resist saying, but he didn't care. There was only the faintest hint of a shrug. I wondered if the reason he'd hung on to them would be in their content. I had no doubt he had read them. There were not many, perhaps half a dozen.

"His address is there," Howard said. "By the way, I didn't read them."

My surprise must have shown in my face.

"Why should I be interested?"

If he was telling the truth it was indicative of how keen he was to get shot of the past. I put the letters in my bag and shook hands with him, knowing I would never see him again, and went out to catch a bus back to work.

Letters, letters, letters, my mind repeated as I found my way on a sort of automatic pilot through the rest of the afternoon, but I didn't open them. I wanted to let some time elapse between that meeting with Howard and the reading of them. I wanted them cleansed. After work I went back to my flat, poured myself a gin and tonic and sat down with the letters on my knee. I had meant to have a meal. To make myself strong. Anyway, the gin strengthened me.

Even so, I wept, the tears falling on the paper that had lost its pristine whiteness with age. These letters were older than I was. It seemed from what I read that the marriage had always been a shaky one, but my father blamed Howard for this.

'*We could have been so happy if he had not been coming and going all the time, bringing you presents and flattering you and treating our home as though he belonged there. Taking your side every time we had a little tiff. Pretending to be my friend.*'

How well I knew the meaning behind those words, 'pretending to be my friend'. Howard had pretended to be my friend, too, and done it so well he had convinced everyone but me.

'*I know I can't ask for the child*,' my father wrote. '*By the time she is old enough to visit me alone it will be too late. I don't want to divide her loyalties*.' And he had added bitterly, and with more truth than he may have guessed, '*Perhaps she won't like Howard, but if I take her from him I take her from you.*'

Now there was no taking to be done. I was twenty-six, and chose to visit the father who had once wanted me. Whether he wanted me now though was another thing.

I spent a miserable few days, coming to terms with what my stepfather had told me, suffering rejection on two counts. At my age, I told myself, I was in need of neither a father nor a stepfather. All the same, I did not find it easy to face the fact that through no fault of mine I had been rejected by both. The girls I worked with were very supportive, and more optimistic than I with regard to looking up my father. One morning when I came in they showed me a letter from a physio asking if there was likely to be a temporary job going at the clinic.

"You're meant to go," they said, smiling at me encouragingly. "It's fate."

I looked at the letter. Sure enough, it was unsolicited. The girl said she was available. Could start right away. There was a telephone number. I rang. "Come in this afternoon," I said. At that moment I made my decision. "If you like the place and us, you can start tomorrow."

I was packed and ready when my friend Rosie rang. "You're going!" she exclaimed. "You're actually going!"

"Tomorrow."

"Golly! Can I come round tonight and say goodbye? I might never see you again." Her voice ran off to a wail. Rosie is heavily into amateur dramatics as well as art.

"Sure," I said. "Any time."

She came in lit up with excitement, eyes sparkling, a new silver beret rakishly balanced over one ear, a slinky black sheath outlining her modest curves, and the masses of Amazonian-looking silver round her neck.

"Hats for evening are in," she explained before I could wipe the surprise off my face. "I'm due at an art show later. So you're off on a father hunt! I never thought you'd do it. Brave old you."

I had felt reasonably courageous until then. Her words scattered my resolve like shot among pigeons, but she was not looking at the newly gutted me. Her eye was taken by the pile of foreign money on the table. "Hey! What's all this? Have you become a millionaire?" She picked up the notes, flicked through them.

"All Italians are millionaires, lire-wise," I told her, using my newfound knowledge learned from the bank teller. "All you need is about £400. But no, there isn't a million lire there. Just enough for a few meals and a bit of room rent."

"He'll ask you to stay. Of course he'll ask you to stay. He's your father, after all."

"*Bon chance*," I said, practicing my almost forgotten French for the stopover in Paris.

"Cor!" she exclaimed, pouncing on the tickets. "You're going Eurostar!" She leafed through them, reading the details aloud, slowly. "Waterloo 1253. Arrive Gare du Nord 1647. Leave by the Gare de Lyons 2009. Arrive Rome 0824. Leave Rome 0915. Arrive Salerno 1217 the next day. Tell me why you're not flying?" She asked the question casually, still gazing down at the tickets as though memorising them, I thought afterwards.

I didn't want to say I needed time to accustom myself to the meeting with my father so I said I wanted to try out the Tunnel, which was also true. Sometimes planes are too quick. They get you to your destination while you're still unprepared. I remembered I hadn't packed my bikini and went to my room to get it. It was nearly autumn but there might be some swimming. Amalfi was a fair distance south. When I returned Rosie was writing on my telephone pad.

"Message for me?" I asked lightly.

She tore the sheet off and crumpled it into her handbag, looking embarrassed. "Just remembered something," she said.

I stood looking out onto the platform at Waterloo watching the passengers hurrying, wondering as one does where they were going, and why. They didn't look much like holidaymakers. There was nobody dressed like me in jeans and denim jacket. Many of them were laden down with luggage. Making perhaps for some smart Paris hotel? The holiday season was pretty well over.

I looked at my watch. Two minutes to go, and I was still the only person in the carriage. This, I said to myself, is how one gets murdered. Obviously I hadn't needed the reservation. The travel company hadn't told me the Eurostars went off half empty. Oddly, though there did not appear to be reservation tickets on the other seats, the one opposite mine had a sticker. Perhaps I should make my way further up and settle in a carriage where there was at least a sprinkling of people. I decided to wait and see if any more passengers came aboard.

There was a shout from the porter. I looked out of the window. A tall man was coming down the platform, moving with an easy stride, swift but unhurried. Smiling. He carried one of those wide, flat bags that weigh nothing and cost the earth. The porter called to him and the man waved casually, as though confident the train would not go without him. Then he swung himself up at the end of the carriage beyond mine and the train began to move. Here comes the murderer. The man booked into the seat opposite me. I looked up at my bag. Should I move?

I heard the door at the end of the carriage open and close. Footsteps, and a moment later he stopped beside me. He glanced at the reservation ticket above the seat. There was laughter in his face as though nearly missing the train was the greatest joke. He swung his bag up on to the rack above and dropped into the seat.

"Hello," he said in the friendliest voice. "We seem to have the carriage to ourselves."

It would have been churlish to say that with the carriage to ourselves he need not take the seat opposite mine. Besides, he was not only extremely attractive, he looked faintly familiar. I wondered if we had met before.

The train was gathering speed. We swept past the suburban stations so fast I could not read their names. I took a paperback out of my bag. He was sitting very erect, watching me. I felt his eyes on my hands, my face, the page. Involuntarily, my eyes lifted. His were dancing.

I said, "With so much space—"

"Yes," he said, breaking in. "It's great. Where are you going?"

"To Paris," I said.

"Oh yes, of course. That's where we're all going for a start. Where then?"

"To Italy." I very deliberately started to read again. Or pretended, because I could not concentrate with him watching me. I glanced out of the window. My! But we were going fast. We were out in the countryside already. I looked down at my book.

"Why not fly?" he asked.

He knew he wasn't disturbing me. He knew I was not reading. "I like trains. Why don't *you* fly?" I riposted, closing my book.

"I like trains, too. I like meeting people. Look who I've met today! I got the jackpot!"

I couldn't help laughing. "You're not English, are you?"

"What makes you ask?"

"Not your accent. It's impeccable." I wondered if I could say it was his infernal cheek and decided against because I couldn't find the right words. I didn't want to insult him. He was clearly well educated and respectable, and there was that drifting consciousness of having met him somewhere before.

"Half Italian," he said. "My father is English. He and my mother don't see eye to eye so she lives in Italy, he in Walton-on-Thames."

"So you're going to Italy too? To see your mother?"

"Not specifically to see my mother. Though of course I shall see her. I have a very convenient assignment. I'm going near to where she lives."

I caught my breath. Journalists had assignments. Before I could speak he said, "I speak French like a Frenchman, too. How's your French?"

"Quite bad."

"Then I could help you through dinner. We have three hours to wait in Paris. There's no food on the train."

"My restaurant French is okay," I snapped. I had remembered why he looked familiar. We hadn't met. But surely he was the man I had seen at the Groucho, standing beside Rosie at the bar when I came in? And again, at a nearby table over lunch. But she hadn't appeared to know him. Hadn't introduced us, anyway.

Hadn't spoken to him. But the Groucho was where media people hung out. Had he been listening to our conversation? Had he rushed back to the office and offered to tail me? The media were interested in my father.

"We might share a taxi?" he suggested.

It was clear there was going to be no shaking him off. I deliberately opened my paperback again and stared at the page. How could he possibly have landed up not only on the same train but in the adjacent seat? There were a number of people who knew I was going to Amalfi, my colleagues at work, my stepfather. Howard! But why should he put a journalist on my trail? He had been glad to get rid of me.

And then I remembered Rosie visiting me last night. Examining my tickets. Writing on my telephone pad. Looking flustered when asked what she was doing. I felt a rush of anger that she should have betrayed me. And then I realised that it was she who had drawn my attention to the article about Andrew Hollis. I had to be grateful to her. How else would I have discovered him? It seemed my stepfather would not have told me. And to be fair, I had not asked her to keep the news to herself.

My companion leaned across and turned a page of my book. I glanced up in surprise. His eyes were merry. "You must have finished that lot," he said. He had a warm personality that expressed itself in the way he inclined towards me when he spoke; the way he used his hands. That was the foreign part of him.

I shut the book, stood up and deliberately turned over the luggage label on his bag. *Carl Beaumont,* I read. *Hotel Maria Convento, Amalfi.*

Chapter Two

I swung round. "So you are going to Amalfi, too!"

He smiled, looking very much at ease. "I have a job to do there," he said.

"What sort of job?"

"I'm a freelance. I do features."

"Are you interested in Ben Tyrill?" I asked bluntly.

He watched me, like a cat. "You know about Ben Tyrill, then?"

I turned my face to the window to hide the colour that was creeping up from my throat. I could see my reflection in the glass, mouth pulled tight and tense, eyes strained. I looked beyond to where the sun shone golden on a field of ripe wheat waiting to be garnered in. The train fled by and there were green fields. It was like flying, on the ground. I had never experienced such speed.

"Who doesn't?" I commented, making my voice light. "He's very famous. You haven't answered my question." It occurred to me that he might have said *touché* and looked at my luggage label if he had not known my name was Jane Hollis and that I was on my way to Amalfi to visit my father. He wasn't hiding anything.

"Of course I'm interested in Ben Tyrill," he said. "Everyone is."

"And is this your assignment? Sussing him out?"

"Not exactly." Again that winning smile.

"What do you mean?"

"Just that. I am not exactly sussing out Ben Tyrill. Let's introduce ourselves, shall we? Miss Jane Hollis. I'm Carl Beaumont from the Southern European News Service. I'm covering your meeting with your father."

"Covering!" My voice rose. "What do you mean, covering?"

As if I did not know. I stared at him, speechless, half sick with worry and shock. *You're following up the Raphael forgery, aren't you?* was what I wanted to say, but I could not because I knew it to be true.

"Ben Tyrill is a news name," he said. "His meeting up with a daughter after twenty-six years is headline human interest stuff. Someone will get the story," he said gently. "Why not me?"

I wondered again, as I had wondered many times since this discovery, what kind of man my father was. Only now I had to relate my interest to the fact that his unexpected, perhaps unwanted, daughter was to arrive armed with her own publicity agent. Unwelcome I might be under ordinary circumstances, but this way I must surely be a hundred times more so.

"Why not you," I echoed, in despair, feeling trapped. "I'm going to find the bar and get a sandwich," I said.

"I'll come with you."

He did, and insisted on paying. I didn't like being in his debt but I had no choice. I thanked him politely and went back to my seat.

The Tunnel was not exciting. I thought they should have it lit up, and why not commission painters to put murals on the walls? That would have given me something to look at. I mustn't read because this is a historic twenty minutes, I told myself. I should remain aware. Of what? A black window. Besides, we might break down. Be blown up by an IRA bomb. The Tunnel might choose this moment to spring a leak. I visualised a marathon swim, with the water getting higher and higher until . . .

Heavens! I was in a state. Taken over by forces beyond my control. The train sped through and emerged in a foreign country where I spoke the language badly. I was going to Italy where I spoke the language not at all. This man, Carl Beaumont, who had stuck himself to me like a leech, wasn't covering my meeting with my father. He wasn't into headline human interest stuff. That was the kind of thing newspapers put their staff reporters on to. I didn't come down in the last shower. He intended to use me to get an interview with Ben Tyrill who is trying to sell a fake Raphael in Amsterdam.

He had moved over to the other side of the carriage, opened

his briefcase and was writing on a large notepad. I would have liked to know what he was writing. Five feet six? Grey eyes? Fair hair, slightly curling, shoulder length? Slim? Wide mouth? Odd-shaped nose? She travels in denim? I was tempted to ask to see what he had written. But no, it could only embarrass both of us. I recognised that he had moved because he didn't want me to see. Naturally.

He closed the pad. "Did you enjoy the Tunnel?"

"No," I said.

I was missing the excitement that came at the beginning of a foreign holiday; a complete lightheartedness that always swung in with the sight of the French coast. Today there was no coast, only further railway lines.

In France it was raining. The train sped on towards Paris. I stared out at the autumn fields. Bedraggled poplars, beaten by the wind, stood yellow and half naked in their straight lines. A small, tired vineyard lay desolate, its few remaining bunches of black grapes abandoned to the approaching cold. We were having a better autumn at home.

I thought: Since some reporter has been trying for weeks, without success, to get an interview with my father, it is possible that he lives in one of those impregnable villas that cling to hillsides in Italy. I had never been to Amalfi but I had seen pictures of it and knew where it sat on the map. It is part of what is usually termed the Italian Riviera, lying in a basin in that range of mountains bordering the Mediterranean, or to be more precise, the Tyrrhenian Sea. And if he does live in an impregnable villa, and he invites me to visit him there, I don't have to take Mr Carl Beaumont with me. And I don't have to tell him anything about our meeting afterwards.

So his Southern European News Service is wasting its money. I felt momentarily cheered.

But if my father failed to invite me to the villa, if he did not wish his present wife – was he married? – to know about me, then he would meet me outside to warn me off. I would then indeed be vulnerable to the Southern European News Service. I began to compose the article. *I witnessed their meeting . . . Jane, tall and slender in her cotton sundress, vulnerable, nervous . . .* I shook the rampant thoughts away. I must, I really must, curb this hysterical imagination.

The rain ceased. I saw his reflection in the wet glass. He was incredibly handsome, I thought again. His black hair – from his Italian mother? – was soft and fell lightly across his high brow. His eyes were Italian, too, large and dark. I wondered what he had from his English father. Height? He must be close on six feet, yet sitting, his head was almost level with mine. Exceptionally long legs? I looked at them. Yes. That's why he sits with knees apart. He is accustomed to having them jammed against seats in front of him. He must be somewhere between twenty-five and thirty, I thought. It was hard to tell.

He wore the look of a man who knows exactly where he is going. Behind his reflection a pale yellow light from the late afternoon sun glowed in the sky. I experienced the defeated feeling I remembered from childhood, of being in the hands of another person. But this man wasn't Howard. He was much more dangerous.

I waited for Paris.

We had dinner at a restaurant of Carl's choice. It was delicious and he a charming host. We were on Christian name terms, inevitably. Carl and Jane. I remember every moment of that evening. He was so attentive, so anxious that I should enjoy myself. If he had not been a newspaper hack – a vulture – I could easily have fallen in love with him. I drank my share of the wine. It helped to smooth the sharp edges of my apprehension. We taxied off afterwards – courtesy of the Southern European News Service, no doubt, as was the dinner – to the Gare de Lyons. The Edinburgh Festival had run away with all my holiday money earlier in the summer. After paying my return fare to Amalfi and buying sufficient lire to last me a week I was pretty well skint.

Of course I had a couchette, he a first class sleeper. We parted. I found my accommodation, lifted my bag onto the bottom berth and waited apprehensively, as one does when travelling alone, to discover who my companions were to be. A swarthy Italian dressed in a dirty T-shirt and grubby jeans came in, scowling, dragging an untidy canvas bag that was as wide as the floor space. He leered at me and addressed me in fast Italian. I indicated with a gesture that I did not speak his language. "English," I said.

"Ah, Inglese." He looked pleased. He pointed to the berth I had appropriated as though, I thought, he might share it with me. I signed that I would sleep above. No, he would not have that. I would sleep there. He glanced above and shook his head. I was beginning to panic.

Two more men came in, both fat, both shambling, their breath smelling of sour wine and garlic. They looked at me with interest. *"Inglese,"* said the first man and they all grinned.

Heavens! I thought. Have we such a reputation abroad? I thought of football hooligans and the so famous *Shirley Valentine*. My watch said five past eight. The train was due to leave in four minutes. I slipped out and went in search of a porter. I found him leaning against a door a little way along the corridor.

"Avez vous un autre couchette?" I asked. An execrable accent I may have but usually I can make myself understood.

He shook his head. *"Complet. C'est complet."* He made flat, sliding movements with his hands, palms down, which I took to mean he was saying in the length of the train there was not another couchette.

I was desperate. "Sleeper?" I asked in English because I did not know the word in French. In his job he should know some English.

Again it was no. *"Complet aussi."*

I fumbled with my handbag, took out my wallet, looked at him hopefully. I had saved something on the taxi. And the dinner. Maybe Carl would be prepared to feed me again. Or maybe I could go without, or live on fruit, or my father might . . . I was wasting my time. The answer was the same, though this time with regret. He looked sadly at the francs, shaking his head. The train began to slide out of the station.

I resigned myself to sitting up all night. I probably wasn't going to sleep anyway. There was too much on my mind. *"Une chaise,"* I said. *"Je prendre une chaise?"*

He understood. He shook his head. *"Complet"*, he repeated and did those palms down movements with his hands again.

I did not notice a man coming towards us until he was close by. I pressed against the wall to allow him to pass.

"Are you all right?" asked a familiar voice.

"No, I'm not," I replied, not looking up at him because I was close to tears.

"What's the matter?"

I indicated the door to my compartment. Carl strode over and looked in, paused only a moment then slid the door open, went inside and emerged with my suitcase. "Come with me," he said and started back down the corridor towards the next carriage.

I followed him meekly. We came to the First Class sleepers. He started looking at numbers. Stopped. Opened a door. Went in and dumped my bag on the floor.

"This is yours?" I asked, making a token protest, feeling guilty at the thought of him taking my place in that compartment with those awful men. The lump of fear in my chest had gone. "Where will you go?"

"This isn't mine," he returned. "Mine's next door."

"The man told me they were all taken."

"I'm sure that's true." He grinned and I saw he was going to leave me to work out for myself how there came to be a sleeper next door to his. It wasn't difficult. He knew from Rosie all the details of my bookings. And he wanted me in his debt. I wasn't about to complain. All right, he had luck on his side. He hadn't arranged for me to be stuck with such dreadful companions. But the luck was mine, also. I was supremely grateful. I could have kissed him. Maybe he was a mindreader. He leant over and kissed me on the lips.

I smiled at him. If he hadn't been a predatory newshound after my story, at that moment I could have been in love with him. "If you need company in the night just bang on the door," he said lightly. *La même chose.* But oh, so very much more acceptable.

I said, "Thank you from the bottom of my heart, but I am accustomed to sleeping alone. I quite like it."

"Glad you got your sense of humour back." He grinned and disappeared.

I did sleep. I lost consciousness virtually as my head hit the pillow. Through my dreams I heard distant voices, a clanking of metal, the secret rattles and tremors that belong with train travel, but none of it disturbed me. The emotional turmoil of the day had taken its toll. When I wakened it was nearly daylight. I looked out of the window and wondered if those were the terracotta rooftops of Florence disappearing behind us. Milano and Bologna would have slid by in the night. Firenze. I practiced the Italian names on my tongue.

I dressed and stepped out into the corridor. He was standing by the window. "We're due in at Rome at eight twenty-four," he said, "and there's an hour to wait, nearly an hour before your train leaves. No time to go anywhere unless you want to break the journey."

"No." I wondered what he meant. I remembered his offer to share my berth last night.

"We had better have breakfast on the station, then. It's not worth checking our bags in for such a short time." We had settled into the easy camaraderie of travelling companions. How could it be otherwise? I tried not to think about the fact that his kindness was double-edged. Thirty per cent for you, seventy for the Southern European News Service who want the dirt about a known faker of old masters thought to be selling a fake Raphael in Amsterdam.

"Penny?"

I jumped. With daylight all my apprehensions had returned. "They're not worth anything. Very ragged," I said.

"You're scared, aren't you?"

"Wouldn't you be?" I nearly added that his presence did not help but I couldn't, remembering the taxi, the dinner, and the horror of having to sleep with those three horrible men. I smiled at him and he smiled back.

The train slid away from the suburbs and on into the country. I looked out at the flat, baked Umbrian countryside, the ancient, barn-like farm houses with their shuttered windows, their walls of wood faggots and logs already stacked for the winter, and thought how different my father's life would be from mine. Even his Italian sky was different. Bluer. Closer, somehow. And the sun was hot, already, on the windows.

"Your papa needs publicity to sell his books."

Lulled into a false sense of security, I was startled by his remark. I felt my nerves tighten. I wanted to say I did not believe the arrival of a discarded daughter at an author's house was of sufficient news value to bring a reporter all this way. I didn't see how it could possibly sell his books. I wanted to say. He's hidden away all these years. Why can't you leave him alone? But I couldn't. This man had an assignment. There was going to be no stopping him.

"I think he has been selling his books very well up till now," I said. "He's very well-known. I don't think he needs publicity."

"Every author needs publicity," he replied. "By the way, I shall be met by my mother in Salerno."

"Oh, right. Good." The relief was enormous. I allowed myself to smile at him.

"Why don't you come with me, first, to her home? My car is there. I can then drive you the rest of the way."

"It's very kind, but I wouldn't dream of bothering you. My seat is already booked on the bus." As if he didn't know.

"It's a nerve-wracking journey going north along the coast from Salerno. The road is narrow and very windy. There's only a low stone wall between you and the rocks below."

"I like buses," I said.

"And what about accommodation?"

"The season is almost over. There will be plenty of rooms vacant," I told him confidently.

He just smiled. We began to approach Rome. I felt the now familiar surge of panic again. We were coming close. When we changed trains we would be on the last lap of the rail journey. Salerno, twelve-seventeen.

I knew immediately when we stepped down onto the platform that the small, elegant, dark haired woman, accompanied by a younger girl, was there to meet Carl. She had that same purposeful air and the same aura of controlled warmth that he wore. The girl was blonde, not in the way an English girl is blonde, with pink cheeks and white skin, but with the firm, creamy skin that one is accustomed to see on Continental beauties, and curious golden-caramel lights in her smoothly flowing hair.

I stood aside at the bottom of the steps, looking up uncertainly as Carl descended, feeling illogically a little lost. The women came forward, both stepping lightly and smiling. Carl greeted them in Italian with pleasure. He put his free arm round the shoulder of each in turn, and kissed them on both cheeks.

"*Mammina*," he said warmly, "you have brought the car!"

"My car," she replied firmly, a little archly, as though now that he was grown up she sometimes forgot that he was her son. "But you may drive." Gracefully, standing with one nyloned knee curved against the other, she lifted a suede handbag and produced a little bunch of keys, dangling them before him. I had the feeling from the way Carl accepted them, with respectful amusement, that this was quite an honour, the driving of Mammina's car.

He drew me forward and introduced us. "This is Miss Hollis," he said. "Jane Hollis. My mother. And Evelina Lambardini." They nodded and shook hands without showing a flicker of interest. The name obviously meant nothing to them. They assumed I was some holidaymaker Carl had picked up on the train. "Jane is going to Amalfi," Carl said. "We can give her a ride."

I saw their disappointment, immediately masked, and said swiftly, "It's quite all right. Really. I would rather like to have a look round Salerno."

The porter had put the luggage down beside us and Carl turned to tip him. He said casually, too casually by half to escape me, "Jane is Ben Tyrill's daughter."

"Ah!" exclaimed Signora Beaumont with a startled look.

"Ah!" echoed the girl, her composure shattered, her eyes alight with interest.

My first reaction was one of anger at his revelation.

"Evelina's father, Antonio Lambardini, is his Italian publisher." He spoke quite firmly and very distinctly, as though explaining to an angry child, and I felt my colour rise in embarrassment.

The girl was looking at me with an intense curiosity that she made no effort to hide. She said, "Come with us. The car is over there."

I had to go, now. I walked limply beside her, and Carl followed behind with his mother.

"This is the first time you have met your father?" Evelina asked conversationally.

So people here knew of my existence? I wasn't a secret? I was dumbfounded. "Yes," I managed.

"You will like him. He is very English. He looks like you."

I turned my head away because my formal smile was crumpling. I was distinctly shaken by this new turn of events. I would have given almost anything to get away now by myself; to spend an hour gnawing my fingernails on a park bench, making up my mind whether to go on or not. The car was an impressive thing, a Lancia. As Carl stowed the luggage in the boot, I made one small, ineffectual protest.

"I feel a little in the way, Carl."

He laid a hand briefly on my arm. "I really can't think why you should. There's plenty of room," he said, and kindly but firmly helped me into the back seat beside Evelina. The car moved off smoothly, purred out into the streets and headed west.

"I hope you will not drive too fast," Carl's mother said and then, as the speedometer needle moved relentlessly round and we were passing one car after another, she spoke sharply to him in Italian. I glanced at Evelina. She was looking down at her small hands, smiling secretly, and I had the feeling she did not mind about speed. I leaned back against the comfortable seat, unrelaxed and nervous.

Nobody mentioned my father again during the short journey to the signora's villa. My new companions were politely formal. They asked me questions about my trip. Where had we changed trains? Paris? So you had dinner there? Was it good? And what of England? Did I live in London? The signora knew London well, of course. They gave nothing away, asked nothing of me.

The tranquil sea came up on our left. We were winding down a smooth cliff road. I gazed out of the window. I don't have to call on my father tonight, I told myself. I don't even have to ring him, assuming I can get hold of the telephone number. Carl will know how to do that. After all, I don't know where the villa is; what it is called. There has to be time to find it. It can't be difficult. That reporter who has been bothering him for three weeks found the way.

Sandstone villas, pinkish in the sun. Terracotta tiles. Geraniums. It was still summer here. I felt uncomfortably warm in the back of the car and wanted to press the button that rolled my window down but did not like to. Foreigners whom I have known all consider the English obsessive about fresh air.

Carl swung the car round, off the main road, and, skirting the edge of the town, headed west. About a mile along the coast he turned sharply right into a drive marked *Privato*, which ran in a half-circle round a clump of tall, dark cypresses. There was a gracious, pillared dwelling built in the pinkish sandstone that seemed to be common to this area.

He said, "Shall I go on in this car?"

His mother shrugged. "You may as well. You will be back?"

"Of course."

She turned round to address the girl. "You will come in with me then, Evelina? Carl will drive Jane to Amalfi."

I began to protest. I felt uncomfortable because there was no doubt I had already spoilt their plans. There was no need for Carl to come with me now. There was a bus from Salerno. But he cut my protestations short.

"I have to go there anyway," he said, and I remembered the luggage label which read, *Hotel Maria Convento, Amalfi*. Evelina stepped out on to the gravel drive. She was speaking to Carl in Italian. He said, "Okay." She rattled on at some length, her voice sharp, then it softened and she leaned over, kissing him on the cheek.

As she straightened she looked directly at me, head held high. "Goodbye," she said.

"Goodbye," I replied.

"Goodbye," Signora Beaumont said. Her tone could not have been more courteous, but disappointment was written plainly on her face. I climbed into the front seat. Carl put the car in gear and sped round the big, circular drive, then out at the front gate.

I said, as we drove along the narrow, twisting road that was carved into the precipitous mountainside, "Why don't you stay with your mother while you are here? It must be less than an hour's drive to Amalfi from her villa." I felt painfully conscience-stricken at what had happened.

"I shall," he replied easily. "But I need a *pied à terre*." He paused, gave me a brief, musing glance, and added, "Remember, I have a job to do."

I said, "I don't want to sound ungrateful, but you're clearly doing this in order to put me in your debt."

He laughed aloud, a very English, hearty laugh. "That is very perceptive of you."

"Then put me down, please, and I shall wait for a bus." I knew he was only being honest, but perversely I was angry with him for it.

"I can't put you down here," he replied. "You might wait hours for a bus. Anyway," he went on reasonably, "it is really no trouble at all for me to drive to Amalfi in this very comfortable car. Why do me out of such a treat? It isn't every day I get the use of it."

"Your mother is very disappointed."

"My mother is wonderful, but she is a little spoiled. She does not understand that money cannot buy people. That is why she is living here and not in Walton-on-Thames with my father."

I was silent a little while, digesting that. "Evelina," I began tentatively. "Is she – er—"

His eyes were on the winding road. "She is a great friend of my mother's."

"And yours, too?"

"Yes," he conceded. "I have known her for a long time."

I turned to the scenery. The hills on our right had grown higher and more grand, until now they rose steeply from the stone wall that guarded the road. On our left, another low wall stood some thirty feet above the rocky shore. As it wound in and out, the road ahead emerged on pleats in the hillside, white and fine and clean, like uneven tacking stitches in one of those dark, gathered skirts the peasant women wore. And down below, where there was room, sometimes a small villa took its chance, riveted to the rocks between road and sea.

Carl asked lightly, "Are we going to be friends?"

He was immensely attractive, sitting there with his dark head erect, his strong hands capably on the wheel; English enough for me to feel at home with him, Latin enough to intrigue. I said nervously, "Not if you upset my father. I mean, if you make things awkward between us. That article in the magazine made his attitude towards the press quite clear."

I thought again of what my stepfather had said: 'This Raphael has been discovered by someone in the Naples area, and they're going to be on to Andrew because that is where he lives.' I clasped my fingers tightly together round my knees. "This is so very important to me"

Unexpectedly he put a hand over mine. It was warm and hard,

and secure. He bypassed my request, saying, "I promise not to race you neck-and-neck to your father's house. In return, I want you to promise to come and look for me afterwards."

"To tell you about it? You can't expect me to do that."

He replied mildly, "You may need someone to talk to. Have you any friends in Amalfi?"

I bit back my anger at his hypocrisy. "You know I have not." Then I retaliated with, "I believe you know more of my father than you will admit."

He shrugged. "I've never spoken to him. He isn't seeing anybody."

"How can he not see *anybody*?"

"Very easily," he said dryly, "as you will observe for yourself when you finally arrive at the Villa Passerina. The garage is on the road, high up, and one enters by a small gate which is usually locked." So he knew the address. Knew where to go.

"To keep the public out?" I asked.

He shrugged again. "Perhaps. Or to keep the children in."

"There are children, then?" Half-brothers, half-sisters of mine? That shook me. I had thought of the possibility, of course, that there were children my father wanted, as well as the one he did not.

"There are always children in Italy," Carl said easily. "But abut this house – you go through the gate and down a very steep, narrow, stone stairway. You enter at the top floor. The villa is hung on the rock between the roadway and their own private beach."

I said, "Tell me about the children. And his wife. You do know, don't you?"

"There are three children. Two girls and a boy. I don't know about them. There were four."

"What do you mean 'were'?" I asked awkwardly, thinking that, in some mind-twisting way, he was including me.

"The eldest boy was killed in a plane crash recently."

I swung round instinctively towards him, horrified. "In July? The plane that crashed in the French Alps and twenty-six people were killed?"

"His eldest son was one of them."

"Oh! How terrible!" I cried in distress. "And the others?"

"They're living with him, I understand."

"Why did you not tell me this before?" I asked, a little defensively. "We could have talked about my father's family on the train. I could have accustomed myself to them a little."

"It's second-hand stuff. I don't know them."

"Evelina has told you?"

"We-ll, yes."

"What sort of woman is my father's wife?"

"I don't know. How would I know?"

"Are you the reporter mentioned in that trade magazine? The one who tried for three weeks to get an interview?"

"No." He was quite definite about that, and I could see he was telling the truth. At that moment we rounded a bend in the road and came upon the town.

"Amalfi," Carl said. He pulled the car in to the side of the road.

We were looking down into a half-moon bay, thickly pin-pricked with golden lights. At the water's edge, street lamps cast a soft glow in the still, dark water. A wide street ran along the front and cars moved idly back and forth.

Carl bent his big frame forward and tapped one finger against the windscreen. "Do you see the curve of the water past the pier, and out towards the point? Now look up."

Chapter Three

I could see the hills folding one against the other so closely that from this distance one was misled into thinking the villas were side by side.

"Take a line straight up between that black patch, that's the tunnel," Carl said, "and the two cypresses, and you'll see on the left a stark white villa with the usual orange-coloured tiles. That's the Villa Passerina. Down below there's a big terrace facing out to sea, though it's mainly hidden by bushes and small trees. It's easier to see at night. It's quite spectacular then with the street lights behind and the lights over the terrace."

I stared and stared hungrily, until after a while I could not see at all because my sight was smudged with tears.

"Well?" Carl said in two syllables, gently, questioningly. We-ll? and suddenly I was unstrung. I forgot that if it were true he was covering my meeting with my father he had almost certainly stopped right here on purpose to get my reaction to the first sight of his home, to which I had never been invited.

"Four children he has brought up," I said. "Four whom he knows well. Why should he be interested in me?"

"Why not?" Carl asked kindly. "You're his flesh and blood. Italians are very family-conscious."

"But he's not Italian. He's English," I protested. I wanted to add: *and he abandoned me, without even seeing me, never got in touch*. I held those emotive words down hard so that they could not escape, dramatically, into the air and make a fool of me.

Carl reached out and put a hand over mine. "He's lived here a very long time. He's got an Italian wife and Italian children."

Half-sisters and brothers from whose company I had been excluded.

"Let's get on, shall we?" He switched on the ignition and put the car into gear.

"I've got to find a room," I said. "How does one go about that?"

"I've booked you into my hotel."

"What!"

He smiled, with his eyes on the road. "You're not very good on your own. Look what happened last night. I took the precaution of making sure you were looked after."

Before he knew what was going to happen last night, I thought cynically, but I was enormously grateful all the same. How could I not be? He was kind, and at the moment kindness was what I needed.

He could not take the car right up to the Hotel Maria Convento. As its name implied, it was an old convent that had been turned into an hotel. Nuns through the ages hadn't had life easy. We left the car and toiled up a line of white-painted stone steps. There is not much one can do with a nunnery, I thought standing on the terrace and looking in through the door, except paint it stark white and hang pretty curtains over the deep window embrasures. It had retained its stone floors and daunting little staircase. Carl went to the desk and checked us in while I looked through an arched window at the astonishing view of the Bay of Salerno with the sun glittering down on the blue water as though it was mid-August instead of late September.

My room, complete with bath, opened onto a balcony. I looked past the telephone and the pretty, tiled floor to see how it had once been a cell in which the sisters lived in spartan circumstances. Stone floor. A hard little bed. The Christ on the Cross, inevitably, remained on the wall at its head but now looked down from a gilt frame. The changes were merely cosmetic: paint and tiles, a wide bed, cosy-looking beneath its flowered duvet, but oh, what a difference!

I was delighted with it and wished I could stay but tomorrow I would have to find a room. I no longer dared hope I would be invited to stay at the Villa Passerina. My journey had taken on a new aspect since my arrival. Since I had exposed myself to Andrew Hollis' home town. Since I had seen how settled in he was. Italian wife. Three children. I felt he would think the arrival of a discarded English daughter no more than confounded cheek. Would he think that the trouble he was in had brought me here out of vulgar curiosity? Would he believe me when I told him I had only today learned his address? There was no gainsaying the fact that he had always known mine. I felt the first stirrings of anger against him, then.

I looked over the balcony. There were tables covered with checked cloths standing on a narrow terrace below, and beyond, a walkway covered with vine. Huge bunches of black grapes hung luscious and tempting. There were several couples seated. A waiter in a white coat came with a tray and put down tiny cups of coffee in front of them. Looking to the left I had a view of the sea and to the right the impressive rock mountain that guarded the town. Over on that hillside was the Villa Passerina. I returned to the room.

Carl poked his head round the door. "How do you like it?"

"Love it," I said warmly. "And thank you so much. But I shan't be able to afford it for more than one night. Perhaps you could tell me how to go about finding a room in the town."

"You're booked in for a week."

"I can't. I'm sorry, Carl, but I can't afford it. I'm sure this dear little nun's cell costs the earth. And as for the meals . . ." I blew out my cheeks, huffing the expense away.

"You mustn't worry. You're not paying," he retorted.

I turned my head. I knew I shouldn't look at him, at the kindness in his eyes, the beauty of his features, his glossy hair, the full upstanding fine-figure-of-a-man of him. I was already in love, which was folly, not to say stupidity. Once he had got his story, once he was home and dry, he would discard me like a wet tissue. I was as much a part of this assignment as that pen and notebook he kept in his briefcase. Don't fool yourself, I said to my treacherous heart. He's probably in love with that girl Evelina, anyway, else why should she accompany his mother today to welcome him?

I tried to see him as a leech, sucking my blood, then dropping away, satiated by his fee. I tried to hate him. I turned to look at him and knew I had failed. I'm just lonely, I told myself in a last desperate attempt. I am a woman alone in the world, whom nobody loves. Loneliness has made idiots of people before now.

"No," I said firmly. "You've been very kind, but enough's enough."

"Let's talk about it tomorrow, shall we?" he asked in his easy way. "I'd like a swim. I presume you've brought a bikini?"

So he disposed of my intention to get in touch with my father today. He knew I wasn't ready.

"Don't you have to take the car back?"

He shrugged. "Not urgently. Mama can use mine."

The water was warm. There were not many people on the beach. Some mothers with pre-school age children. The older ones would be back at school. And several elderly couples who might have been Scandinavian. One obviously English, scarlet-skinned from sunburn, his hair tied back with a rubber band and granny glasses on his nose. I swam out some distance then trod water, looking up at the steep hill where Carl had pointed out the Villa Passerina.

There was a jumble of houses and for a moment I could make out nothing exceptional. Then gradually, as my eyes became accustomed to the lines of wall and brick and rooftop tiles, I saw it: whitewashed, with green shutters, set so closely into the earth that it seemed almost part of the cliff face. And there was its private beach, below. From here I could see a winding path, probably steps, leading from the vine-hung terrace and a sort of covered way down through a steep garden into a little bay. I wondered if my father had made the money to pay for all that magnificence by painting fakes. Copies, I corrected myself. It was perfectly legal to paint copies.

It was a peaceful, settled scene. I thought again about the disruption I could cause. For the first time I wished I hadn't come.

Dinner was served outside in the cloisters. "Thirteenth century," said Carl, "and founded by Saint Francis of Assisi." It was dark now. Had become dark in that sudden, southern way, dispensing with the twilight to which we are accustomed. Flickering candles lit the small tables with their bright red and yellow cloths. In the centre stood a well, surrounded by pots of geraniums. A magnificent creeper with purple flowers trailed over the wall. Above, floodlit against the sky and ringing out the hour, was a singularly musical bell in a square tower with a tall, cone-shaped roof.

We had *stracciatella*, a Roman soup, Carl told me; rich, creamy and delicious, with threads of egg swimming in it like thin gold fish. It was served steaming hot from an enormous tureen with a great silver ladle.

"I'll choose the meal," he had said, taking the menu with his air of easy authority.

I said, trying to laugh about it and thinking tears were more suitable, "My lack of moral fibre seems to have put me at your mercy. What is to happen now?"

Carl said reflectively, "A reporter has to be something of an opportunist, Jane, but don't think me insensitive. Part of me stays outside my work."

"Can you really believe the public is interested?" I asked.

"The public likes human interest stories, you know that." Carl raised his dark brows and gave me a quizzical look. Then he said lightly and yet at the same time gently, "I have taken you on. I am going to look after you. It's a toss-up between my company and being on your own, and being on your own isn't good enough tonight, is it? Be honest with yourself, Jane."

That extraordinary personal magnetism! One moment, I could be furious with him, the next, eating out of his hand.

But I was really furious with him on another level, for persistently carrying on this pretence about covering my meeting with my father when I knew very well he was on the track of the Raphael. I tried to broach the subject. I looked at him. Looked away. I thought, if I accuse him of lying to me and he takes offence . . . Some frightened core in me was causing me to cling to him. I didn't understand myself as one does not when one is falling in love. And this wine isn't helping, as it did last night, I thought. Considering I had downed two and a half glasses on an empty stomach it was surprising that I still felt distinctly sober.

He ordered veal. It came with almonds and an almond liqueur sauce and tasted delicious. Then he insisted on an ice. It was a wonderful meal. I thanked him, awkwardly. It is not easy to find the right words when one knows a man isn't paying, that this expensive meal came out of his expenses, and what is more, you are the bait that has been offered up to his paper for these very expenses.

The moon had come up. It was nearly full. It shone down on the cloisters. The white pillar cast black shadows.

"Would you like a walk down into the town?" he asked. "Or do you want to go to bed?"

Of course I wanted to take a walk, but not with him, in the soft night, with the light-studded hills around, and the smell of the sea. I would challenge almost anyone to stay aloof from his sort of charm in those circumstances.

"I'd like a coffee. No, I don't want to walk, thanks," I said. "Just a coffee. Shall we go inside? It's suddenly a bit cool. Then I'll probably go to bed. Do you mind?" I pushed my chair back. I was suddenly determined to find a way to introduce the Raphael picture. It was bound to be easier to broach the subject here than breathlessly climbing steps, in any case, notwithstanding the moon and stars and smell of the jacaranda.

"I shall mind very much," he replied giving me that friendly, quizzical look that must have been melting female hearts since he was a child. "But do let's go in. We can't have you getting cold."

We walked down a passageway with plain, white-painted vaulted ceilings, long, cushioned sofas and high-backed rocking chairs. On my left, small pillars supported more arched windows that looked out on the bay. Here, the clever architects had conjured up a guest lounge, elegant, strange, and still retaining the stark look of a convent corridor.

"This will do nicely," Carl said, gesturing towards a window seat. He was entirely unperturbed, as though he had suggested the coffee, and not the walk.

We stayed there for half an hour or more, watching the other guests come and go, talking desultorily, drinking our coffee. As time went by my nervousness abated, as no doubt he intended. He knew I had something to say.

I blurted out, "It's the Raphael, isn't it? That's why you're here." I hesitated while I tried to pluck up courage to say the rest, that he wasn't covering the human interest story of me, the long-lost daughter, meeting Ben Tyrill. I felt dreadfully vulnerable. I needed to talk. The wine had loosened my tongue. Don't talk, I said to myself. Don't tell him anything. But my need for a friend at that moment was greater than my resolution.

We stared at each other, I into his melting eyes, feeling my treacherous heart melt also; he concerned and kind as though he had nothing to apologise for.

"Shall we talk about it?" he asked. He put a hand over mine. It was warm and comforting. "What do you know about your father's past?" he asked.

"Nothing. I know there has been talk in the papers about this picture, but not knowing who Ben Tyrill was, even if I had read it I wouldn't have been interested."

"You didn't know Ben Tyrill was your father?"

"Nobody told me." I heard the resentment in my own voice and offered a weak smile as cover. "Andrew Hollis is the man I understood to be my father and he was missing. Had been missing all my life. He left, it seems, because my stepfather wouldn't go away."

I wasn't going to tell him the intimate details I had read in the letters that had made me cry. "My stepfather told me he was involved in – was connected with someone who—" I didn't want to repeat what Howard had told me. His story was likely to be biased. I wanted to know what the world knew, which was what Carl could tell me, he being a journalist. "I'd be grateful if you would tell me about it," I said. "Tell me a bit about this forgery business." I didn't trust my stepfather to have told me the truth. And anyway, he had told me very little.

"All right. There have been four big art forgery cases over the past twenty years," Carl said, leaning back, hands in pockets, staring at the ceiling. "There was a Dutchman who turned out five Filippino Lippis, a Frenchman who produced three almost perfect Titians and sold them for a fortune to an American millionaire, and an Englishman who was painting away in the fifties in an attic in the Midlands and flooding the market with Tintorettos, van Dycks and Salvator Rosas. And there was Ben Tyrill, or Andrew Hollis as we know him to be. The other three have each done a stretch in jail, but they're free now. My agency has a man assigned to each of them."

"And you got the plum assignment." I tried to sound careless, or rather, uncaring, but the bitterness crept into my voice. "You got an abandoned daughter thrown in."

Carl did not reply. He signed to the waiter to bring more coffee.

"What are you going to do?" I asked.

"Talk to him, if I can."

"And if you can't?"

"I am a reporter. It's my job to search for facts. It is rather surprising, don't you think, that he should have come back into the art world after all these years?"

"Just at a time when a forgery is being unloaded on the market? Very surprising," I agreed, hoping the sarcasm didn't sound too awful. "You don't credit him with much intelligence."

"I am not judging him," Carl replied. "Merely looking for the facts."

"I can't help you with facts," I said. "Money spent on my dinner is money badly invested," I added then regretted my ungraciousness and smiled at him.

"You don't know that your father was suspected of selling forged old masters in his London gallery?"

"Yes. I've heard. And his partner committed suicide. Yes, I know that. My stepfather informed me. But my father was acquitted."

"His guilt wasn't proved," Carl corrected me. "He was quite a well-known faker."

"What is a faker? What does he do that's different from ordinary artists who make copies?"

Carl leaned back in his seat, stretching, smiling faintly to himself. I thought again how incredibly handsome he was and what a good face he had. If ever I had seen right-thinking stamped on features, it was there. And yet, how could he be doing right in digging out a man to, at the very least, make a public spectacle of him? A man who wanted to remain private. At the worst, get him taken to court, fined, maybe jailed?

He said, "There are techniques for ageing paper and ink. A good faker will know how to imitate collectors' marks. They know how to build up layers of authentic-looking varnish that is very difficult indeed to verify."

"How?"

He laughed. "I don't know how, but gossip has it that quite common foodstuffs can be used. Honey. Sugar. Cheese. Eggs. They go to no end of trouble. Of course they do. The profits can be enormous." His expression became whimsical. "If they don't end up in jail."

"Why are they saying this picture that's surfaced in Amsterdam is a fake?"

"It's only an opinion. Auctioneers and fine art dealers are supposed to be experts, but in the long run you're having to rely on their opinion."

"They may be wrong."

He smiled at me. "Of course." He leaned forward and took my hand again. "It's still a news story, Jane. If the picture is an authentic Raphael it will go for monopoly money. That's one good story. If he's trying to pass off one of his fakes, that's a second good story. And his long-lost daughter is a story in herself."

I snatched my hand away. He managed to look sad. "Listen," I said, "surely all the Raphaels are known? They've been around for four or five hundred years."

He shrugged. "Raphael painted about two dozen portraits, of which some are doubtful attributions. And some are no longer extant. There are the Madonnas. He painted a series of them. Who knows? There's a story behind it, as I said."

"This picture could be one of those, as you say, no longer extant."

"Sure," he replied in his easy, smiling way. "Sure. Why not?"

"I don't see why an artist shouldn't amuse himself making up egg mixtures or whatever, anyway."

"Of course. Nothing wrong with that, providing he doesn't sign his picture with the artist's name."

"And had he done that, when he was drummed out of London?"

"As I said, his guilt wasn't proved." We looked at each other across the coffee cups. My face was tight with apprehension. He looked somehow resigned. Not guilty, though, as a man should be who was out to expose someone.

"So what about this picture? Why should it have come from Andrew Hollis? It was offered anonymously. If the media know only that it came from this area then it must have been offered anonymously. It's the newspapers stirring up trouble again, isn't it? Look what they've done to the poor old Royal Family." Look what you're proposing to do to me and this father of mine, I wanted to add, but my feelings were getting out of hand and my emotions becoming muddled. I'd lost track of whether I believed one thing or another. I was just angry, and frightened.

"A bit different," he demurred.

"What?"

"From the Royal Family." But he smiled, humouring me. Then he rose.

"You must be tired," he said. He spoke kindly, ignoring my question. "I expect you would like a reasonably early night."

"I'm sorry," I said quickly. "I'm sorry for being so rude." I even found myself stretching out a hand to hold him.

He shook his shoulders back, pushed his hands down into his pockets and jingled some coins. "I told you," he said good-humouredly, "even unwelcome company is sometimes better than none. You have had a pretty hectic time, though." He bent down, took my outstretched hand and kissed it. "Goodnight, Jane. Sleep well."

I had had enough of trying to sleep. I opened the shutters on a glitter of pale blue ocean, an idling yacht and two small fishing boats. It was a perfect morning, the sky cloudless, with the sun bathing the house-cluttered hillside opposite in a wash of pink. I went out onto my little balcony. Instinctively, my eyes turned to that steep hill above the bay where Carl had pointed out the Villa Passerina.

I must have stood there for a long time, leaning on the balcony rail in my dressing-gown, lost in my private world of apprehension, until two workmen in plain blue overalls came swinging down the road, conversing volubly at the tops of their voices, bring me back to the present with a rush. I went inside, and began to dress. I would walk, I decided, until a reasonable hour, and then I would go straight to the villa. Walking might serve to calm me, and if I were away from the hotel before Carl returned, there was little chance of his finding me.

There were only servants in the foyer, black-clad women with their hair dragged tightly into small buns at the back of their heads. They leaned on their brooms and mops when they saw me, smiling and nodding their *buon giornos*. I let myself out by the heavy wooden door that led onto the terrace, then took the steps down to the road. I turned inland at the square, past the cathedral, the closed shops, the *ristorantes* with their spiced smells, the dark, arched doorways, and coming to the top of a hill, found myself looking down on a grassy, rocky slope with a valley snaking away below. This, I told myself, would be a good enough place to walk and hide.

I remember little about that walk except the time, measured in fevered glances at my wristwatch, that told me it was seven when I left the town, and a quarter to ten when I returned. I came back hurriedly, not looking at anything or anybody in the busy streets; suddenly it seemed too late, and my father might have gone out for the day. I went through the narrow, dark passages at the back of the shops, because Carl might by this time have returned, discovered my flight and come after me. I came out close to the tunnel where the road ran up the hill, cross-slanted with shadows from the morning sun. Ignoring the sign directing pedestrians round the footpath promontory, I walked instead up through the cold, dark tunnel, breathing in the petrol fumes as cars fled shrieking through.

The entrance to the villa was only a few hundred yards past the tunnel. An iron gate in the wall, that was all, and a locked garage. The gate was locked, too. I could see no bell. I stood there undecided for a moment. There was no sign of life in the garden below. I climbed over the gate and guiltily, and very nervously, began the descent. I could see nothing of the villa from here, only steps and a trellis, a lot of vines, a terraced garden with beautiful, golden canna lilies, some tall earthenware jars with geraniums trailing from them, and a low pink wall. The only movement was a scurrying brown lizard at my feet.

I wended my way downwards, and came to a blue-tiled terrace outside a narrow wooden door. There was a bell here, and a chain hanging from it. I took my courage in both hands and gave the chain a gentle pull. The villa sprang to life. There was a cry from behind the door, a voluble stream of Italian, then footsteps, and the door opened, bringing me face to face with a plump, middle-aged woman with thick black hair, black velvety eyes, and a white apron tied round her vast middle where her waist should be. She looked at me in surprise. "*Buon giorno.*"

Then, as I replied haltingly, "*Buon giorno—*"

"*Un' Inglesina*! How did you get in?"

"I climbed over the gate," I admitted sheepishly.

She shook her head and wagged a finger angrily at me. "There is a bell. We will have to make it easier to see. Or make the gate higher. What do you want?"

I smiled tentatively because, despite the anger, she was obviously kind. "I want to see Mr Hollis," I said.

She raised her black eyebrows and clicked her tongue, exasperated by my request. "English reporter?"

"No," I said. "I am not a reporter."

"The *Signore* see nobody. Go away. *Presto*!"

"Tell him," I ventured, "it is Jane."

"Jane? Who is Jane?" She waited.

Could I risk telling her the truth? I didn't have a chance to decide. She had got bored with my indecision. She burst into a flood of incomprehensible Italian and waved me back towards the gate. I panicked and blurted out, "I must see him. I have come all the way from England to see him." And then, because the door moving relentlessly towards me was nearly closed, "I am his daughter."

That did it. She indicated the steps behind me with a contemptuous sweep of her arm, and shut the door in my face.

I stumbled back through the garden, numb with misery. The gate came up before me. I didn't feel capable of climbing back over. I turned and looked at the villa, or rather its roof and the part of the steeply sloping garden that was within my view. I considered going back and waiting, sitting under a tree until someone came out. I might have done it, except that Carl came round the corner. I tried to pull myself together. Tried to climb over the gate. My legs were like jelly, and shaking. I gave up. He was walking swiftly, hands in his pockets, frowning. He came right up to me and stood looking down at me across the gate. I couldn't speak.

He said, "So it wasn't a great success! Here, let me help you." Even a dangerous enemy can look like a friend when you're seriously distressed. I tried again to climb over the gate and with his help managed it. If he had held out his arms at that moment I would have gone into them. But he didn't. He led me back down the hill, hurrying me with his long strides. "Have you had breakfast?"

"No."

"Too busy getting away from me. You'd cope better if you had paused at least for a cup of coffee. There's a trattoria down the hill a little way."

"I'm sorry," I said. It was all I could manage. He did not reply.

The trattoria, like everything else along this bit of coastline, was set into the cliff, with windows down the seaward side. We sat at a little round table in the far corner, and an enormously fat man in a white apron that stretched from his chest to his knees served us with coffee and biscuits.

The coffee was strong and hot, and there was a lot of sugar in it. I found it comforting. Calmed, I told Carl what had happened. A tabby cat came and rubbed itself against my legs, looking longingly at the empty cups. I said, "I've got to see him."

"Of course. The fact that your father and mother agreed to part all those years ago does not affect the grown-up you. Of course you must see him. And you shall." He doodled on the table with a spoon. "We will have to make a plan," he said. "We should have made it yesterday. I knew the villa was shut and barred to casual visitors, and so did you. It didn't occur to me that you would run away."

"I'm sorry," I said again. I was too upset to think of plans.

"Do you water-ski?"

"I thought you were cooking up a plan," I said defensively.

"I am. My plan involves a bit of water-skiing."

"Sorry," I repeated.

"There's this chap called Enrico Bertini who has a motor boat and hires out skis. Why don't you take a few runs, then conveniently fall in by the private beach?"

My heart leapt. Then I realised that this might only lead to a repetition of this morning's fiasco. "Even if he were on the beach, he could still get back inside the villa before I had swum in."

"Oh yes. It's not a foolproof idea, but it's something to work on. You could also write him a letter, which he might throw into the wastepaper basket. On the other hand, he may not. Perhaps that depends on how good you are at writing letters." He calmed me, cheered me, and injected a needful spirit of hope into me. I forgot that he was a journalist. I forgot everything but the fact of my own distress. Later, I came to think that his training had taught him to show only the side of himself that he wished to be seen, but at that moment I was too grateful for his company, his sympathy and help to be critical.

We returned to the hotel and collected our swimming gear, then hurried to the beach. We went down some steps onto the sand and wended our way between the fishing boats. There were nets stretched out to dry, and the air was full of the smell of sun-dried sea life and salt. There was no sign of Bertini. Carl did not know where to find him. We swam, then ate a seafood lunch at one of the little cafés on the waterfront.

"Bertini?" echoed the waiter when Carl asked. "He will be here. Every day he comes, though there is not much work for him now. It is late in the season. Perhaps he takes the siesta." The man came back later to say that one of his colleagues had told him Bertini's sister was ill and he had taken her to the hospital. He would not be back until five o'clock. "You want the water-ski?"

Carl nodded. "But five o'clock will be too late."

"You make arrangements, and ski in the morning. He will be here for sure because it is Saturday."

We had to be content with that. "I shan't be here tomorrow," Carl said, "but I'll fix it up for you."

I thought, this is odd, very odd. Here he is sending me off to meet my father on my own. After what had happened earlier I naturally assumed any plan he came up with would include him. We lay on the sand baking in the sun, swam, walked round the rocks, then lay in the sun again. The afternoon slid by. We came back to the beach at five o'clock and there was Bertini dozing in his little fibreglass motorboat as it rocked gently on the water. Carl had explained that he spoke no English. Any communications between us would have to be in sign language. Meanwhile, he gave the instructions. And handed over a wad of notes. I knew there was no point in trying to appear independent. Anyway, I was becoming very cool about his expense account.

"Tell him I'm very out of practice," I said. "I don't want any zig-zagging. Straight out, a loose turn, then in to the beach."

He conveyed that information, laughing and looking stern by turns. I gathered Bertini liked to play tricks. We walked back to the hotel. He said, "I have to leave you now. I must return my mother's car and pick up my own. It's a little less impressive than the Lancia but it gets me around."

And see that Italian girl Evelina whom his mother has chosen for him, I thought. I'd bet that was why she had waved him on instead of telling him to get his own car out of the garage. So that he would be obliged to return.

"I'll be back tomorrow," he said. "Okay?"

"Okay," I said, still baffled that he should disappear having set me on the road to meeting my father. I could only assume he had a more sophisticated plan than the obvious one of muscling in.

Chapter Four

I came down to the beach at the allotted time of ten o'clock. Bertini was there, the little fibreglass motorboat rocking gently on the water. We greeted each other. "*Buon giorno.*" He lifted the water skis out and handed them to me. I stepped into the shallow water to put them on while he climbed back into the boat, sending up a little prayer that I was going to be able to manage. I hadn't been on skis for a couple of years. Bertini was hunched over the controls. The engine burst noisily to life. He turned his dark head, grinned and raised one thumb. I firmed my grip on the tow rope bar, crouched ready, then the boat shot forward in a spray-filled leap and the rope jerked in my hands. I was away, skimming across the water. Bertini glanced round to make certain I was all right. I was, triumphantly so, my senses singing with a familiar exhilaration that was part fear, part excitement, part pride, because a full half-minute had passed and I was still upright.

The little boat swung away from the waterfront, turned left and made a circuit of the bay, then sped inshore. Bertini knew his job. He swung out, swung back, swung out again and I caught my breath. If he didn't stop I was going to take a dip. He came straight in then. We were less than a hundred yards from the boatshed at the bottom of the Villa Passerina garden. I flung my arm in abandonment and sank beneath the turbulent waves that churned in the wake of the boat. When I emerged from the water, gasping, I saw the boat was speeding on. Then I heard the engine being throttled down, and it went silent.

One of my skis had come off. I managed to unclip the other one and swam in on my back, supporting them. There was a tiny beach, a platform of rocks and, adjoining the boatshed, a stone ramp running up from the water. I pushed the skis ashore then pulled myself carefully onto the sun-hot smooth stone, looking round nervously. There was a folded sun umbrella lying by the boatshed, a stone seat and footprints in the sand. Above, the bushes blocked my view. There was nothing to see of what I knew to be a cliff and then the terraced garden.

I squeezed the salt water out of my hair, drew my knees up under my chin and circled my legs with my arms. I stared down into the water, feeling a little scared, recognising for the first time that to trespass like this was both discourteous and undignified. Certainly I could not walk up through the garden and present myself, semi-naked and wet, at the villa. Besides, I might be here for days before somebody came down. Why had it not occurred to me that this plan was fraught with potential failure? Then I remembered that it had. Presumably Bertini had been briefed to wait for me. Carl had not translated his instructions. Did it matter if I had to sit here all day? The sun was warm. My bikini would soon dry.

An hour must have passed. Easily an hour. I began to think they had seen me from the villa, coming in, seen Bertini out on the water, closed the shutters, locked the doors. "It's that girl the maid sent packing yesterday."

My apprehensions were getting the better of me. I thought of giving the project up, of waving to Bertini and beckoning him in. He was perhaps half a mile away, a mere lump in the boat as he bent, presumably, over the engine. I began to wonder if, after all, he did have engine trouble.

Suddenly there were children's voices. Involuntarily, my head came up and I swung round. They were coming closer, lively, round-vowelled Italian voices rising to crescendos of amusement, dipping in consternation, interest, alarm, readable as music and as entertaining.

The children burst through the bushes, a small blonde girl who could not have been more than five years old, and a sturdy, black haired boy. They saw me and stopped, suddenly shy. There was a protest from someone behind and they jolted reluctantly forward. Another girl, considerably older but still a child, came round the bend in the path, head craned, eyes curious. She looked Italian, this one. She had an olive skin and those velvet Italian eyes. They stood in a huddle, staring at me.

"Hello," I ventured.

"English!" That was the eldest, the last in the line.

I stood up then. "Yes, I am English," I told them. "Who are you?"

They came forward, the little one friendly as a kitten. She had the fairest of fair skins and her hair curled just a little like that of an English child. "This is our private lido." She said it kindly, as though I had made a wholly excusable mistake.

"I am very sorry. I took a tumble off my skis." I nodded towards them where they lay on the flat stones.

The boy went straight over, looking down at the skis with interest. "They're Enrico's." Then he glanced up towards the little boat now by far into the bay. "Why doesn't he come back for you? Has he broken down?"

"I suppose so."

"Then how will you get back?"

"I expect he will come and get me when he can."

The boy said politely, "We don't mind, but Father doesn't like people coming in."

I took the bull by the horns. "Are you Mr Hollis's children?" I asked.

They nodded, all together. The eldest, the tall girl, asked curiously, "Do you know him, then?"

"I – er – I know a lot about him," I said, a little shaken because these were my half-sisters and brother I was talking to, and this was a poignant, memorable moment for me. Yet I had to stay calm. I said, "I would like to know him. Does he ever come down here?"

"A reporter came onto the lido," the boy said. "Our father was very angry. You're not a reporter, are you?"

"No," I replied swiftly, "I am not a reporter." Then I added: "Tell me your names."

"I am Marisa." The tall girl nodded her head towards the boy. "That's my brother Guido."

"I am Lucia," chimed in the smiling one. "I'm five. I am small for my age."

I smiled back. "Indeed you are, Lucia." I had little knowledge of five-year-olds, but this child was diminutive. I stared at her, hungrily looking for some resemblance to myself. Her colouring was the same, but her features were still unformed. The elder girl had a short, straight nose that could be said to resemble mine. "You all speak English very well," I told them.

"Our father is English." That was Guido, matter of factly.

"And your mother?"

"Italian," said Marisa.

"Our father comes from London," Lucia offered in a sing-song voice so that I suspected this was her party piece, "and our mother comes from Rome. She's Roman, like Julius Caesar. And he's English, like a rose."

I laughed appreciatively, and they laughed, too. The family joke evidently wore well. They told me Marisa was twelve, Guido nine. And the fat maid who had scolded me was called Maria. She came from Naples but only went back once a year to see her family. She had a son called Nino who did odd jobs like gardening and cleaning shoes.

I asked them tentatively if they had ever been to England. There was silence then. Word-packed silence. Lucia wriggled, glanced at Marisa. Guido knitted his dark brows, and his mouth drooped at the corners. Marisa drew a long sigh of a breath, as though the responsibility of being the eldest and the spokesman weighed heavily on her shoulders. "We had a brother who was at school in England," she said. "He had an English name. Leslie. When he was flying home for the holidays they crashed."

I had not really thought seriously about this boy as my half-brother before, on the journey down. Now, standing in my father's garden, surrounded by these half-English children, I felt connected and was touched by a cold sense of loss.

"I am sorry," I said. "I am sure you three must be a great comfort to your parents."

Lucia nodded. The others were silent.

"Your father writes books," I said. "I have seen them. I would like to meet him. Is he likely to be coming down here this morning?"

Marisa regarded me with interest, her dark head on one side. "Why do you want to meet him?"

I cast round swiftly for a suitable answer. "Because he is

English – and an interesting man. Does he come down here to bathe?"

Yes, he liked to swim, they said.

I glanced up and saw Bertini had given up the pretence of fixing the engine. He was lying back in the boat, his face turned up to the sun.

"Look," I pointed out, "Bertini seems to have mended the engine. Would you like a ride in his boat?"

They nodded eagerly.

"Would your parents mind?"

"They won't know, will they?" That was Guido.

"Mightn't they see you from the villa?" I asked, hoping it would be possible.

Marisa said mischievously, "It will be too late then, won't it?"

But not too late, perhaps, for my father to come down here and call them in. I stood up and waved. Bertini waved back, moved forward in the little boat and the next moment the engine burst to life. We gathered on the landing stage waiting for him, the children's faces bright with excitement. The boat sped towards us, Bertini cut the engine and it drifted in.

"Tell him we would like a run round the bay," I suggested to Marisa. "He doesn't speak English, as you no doubt know."

She handed the message on, and Bertini replied in a flood of good-natured Italian. Guido held on to the stern of the boat while we climbed aboard and then he jumped in after us. Bertini started the engine again and the little craft leaped forward. Lucia gave a shriek of delight and grasped my hand.

We did two circuits of the bay, then came in within a hundred yards or so of the lido. I managed to make Bertini understand I wanted the engine stopped. He and the children chatted animatedly. I turned to face the villa and noted that there was a man standing on the balcony, looking this way.

"That is probably your father looking out," I said, trying to make my voice casual. "Why don't you wave to him?"

They all waved. Guido put his hands round his mouth, giving a loud, bird-like cry that would carry right up the hillside.

"That's Guido's special call," Marisa said to me. "Our father will know it's us."

Evidently he did, for he turned and immediately disappeared. I signed to Bertini to circle the bay once more, and then, I thought, we must go in. There was a woman standing on the rocks as we swung back.

Lucia said, "There's Mama," and I could tell by her expression of pleasurable anticipation that my father's wife was not in the habit of chastising them for such indiscretions as going out with a local boatman. I felt nervous as we came in. I had to speak to this woman. I would start by apologising, and leave the rest to chance.

The children called to her in Italian as soon as the engine cut out, and she replied, shaking her head and gesticulating prettily, obviously admonishing them in as stern a manner as she thought fit. Guido spoke indignantly, pointing to me, and his mother laughed. I caught the word, "*Inglesina*".

As we drifted towards the rock ledge I called, "I am sorry if I worried you. I was talking to the children and offered them a ride. They were perfectly safe."

The woman was plump, with curves in all the right places. She had very black hair, swept off her face and curling softly round her ears. Her features were good, her eyes dark and very large, her mouth gentle, and there was the curve of a much younger woman in her cheeks. She was wearing a pale green dress with a small, neat collar and no sleeves. She said, speaking with only the faintest trace of an accent, "It was kind of you to take them, but they were naughty to go. Their father is not pleased. You will understand they should not go out with strangers."

"Of course," I replied. "I do understand. I am very sorry." I jumped ashore with them, talking quickly, explaining how I had lost the tow rope and come here earlier. I moved slowly towards my skis, bent slowly to pick them up, wondering what I could say with the children listening. I had to say something, otherwise the work of the morning would be wasted.

She made it easy for me, after all. She spoke to the children in Italian then turned to me. "Marisa is late for her music lesson. I must hurry her away. And Guido was to go down to the town on an errand for his father." They thanked me gaily then, miraculously, they set off at a run for the steps with Lucia after them, leaving me alone with my father's wife.

I had half-lifted the skis from the rocks. Now I put them down again and turned to her. She was staring at me with a startled look on her face. "I would like to see your husband," I said.

"I know." The startled look went and she spoke kindly, gently. "I see now that you are Jane. Maria told me. And oh, my dear, you are so like my husband! I would have known those grey eyes anywhere. And Marisa's mouth! Not my husband's mouth, but Marisa's. You two must have it from an ancestor."

Suddenly I felt warm, and foolishly shaken because she had spoken of me as family.

"I am sorry Maria should have sent you away," she went on, "but those were her orders, to get rid of anyone, absolutely anyone, who wanted to see Andrew." She smiled. "Maria came to me and told me with great indignation that an English girl had tried to get in by pretending to be Andrew's daughter. I knew immediately it must be you. And I knew you would come back, but I did not tell him because—" She broke off, then said impulsively, "Of course he must see you, my dear. You are his, and your mother is dead. Of course you must come to us."

I was overwhelmed by her kindness, her gentle courtesy. I said, "So he knows?"

"He gets the English papers. Yes, he knows. We were very sorry about your loss."

"Then why did he not write?" I asked.

She looked down at her hands. An enormous ring, silver with some gleaming yellow stone, was on her second finger. She said, "He is not himself."

"Is he ill?"

"No, he is not ill. But he is worried. Our eldest boy died in July."

"I am so sorry."

"Andrew wanted Leslie to go to his old school. And Guido. He wanted them to have an English education. Now, he feels that—" She broke off, hesitated, then started again, speaking slowly and thoughtfully. "There has been so much trouble connected with England, and all the time he has lived abroad everything has gone well. We have been so happy.

"He was very, very bitter when I first met him. I have softened him, and helped him to forget. And gradually, I brought him back to the work he loves. To art. You know about that trouble?"

I nodded.

"They did this terrible thing to him. They hounded him and brought him to court for selling old master fakes. As if he would!" she exclaimed loyally. "He is the most honest man in the world. They couldn't prove anything. His partner committed suicide, too. That was dreadful for him."

"Was his partner guilty, then?"

She shrugged. "Andrew will not say. 'The man is dead,' he says. It is pointless, you understand, to declare a dead man guilty or innocent."

"Then why did he commit suicide?"

"Andrew says he had a progressive disease, but the doctors were able to control it. Then this upset, the shock and the trouble, made him very ill. It happens sometimes. Shock can do dreadful things to a person, Jane. Andrew says he committed suicide because he knew he was going to die. He didn't want to spend his last few months on earth the way Andrew spent his last few months in England. And who can blame him?"

"And my fa – your hus—" I broke off. "What do I say?"

She smiled. It was the warmest, kindest smile in the world. "You are grown-up, and a stranger. You have to start from the beginning. One cannot have a grown-up stranger calling one 'Father'. Why don't you call him Andrew? And I am Donna."

I was deeply touched. They said Italians loved their children. It seemed they could love other people's children, too.

Bertini was rocking sleepily in his little boat on the green water. I turned back to Donna. "And Andrew is back in the art world now?"

"Yes."

"Why did they suspect him?"

"Because he is a very good copyist. He says that himself. But he would never try to pass one of his copies off as genuine. His gallery in London had several old masters which some people thought dubious. But the difference between an old master and a fake is only an opinion."

Wasn't that what Carl had said?

"Recently," Donna continued, "there has been trouble in New York over a Cassatt bought by an American years ago. He put it back on the market and it was pronounced not authentic. The person who had authenticated it years ago is now dead. The man who has taken her place has a different view. It is all a matter of personal opinion," she repeated.

She turned and indicated the stone seat where the boathouse cast its shade. "Let's sit down. There is so much to talk about." We crossed to the seat and sat side by side. "Andrew is not much of a talker. I must tell you a little about him. And there may be questions you want to ask. What brought you here, so late? That stuff in the papers?" She spoke of it disdainfully.

"Yes."

"He will be hurt. You must be prepared for that. He is touchy about this publicity. You will have to reassure him your coming is not due to idle curiosity. He has never said, but I have always felt he was hurt that you did not look him up when you came of age."

I retorted sharply, "He might have sent his address. It would have been a help."

She looked astonished. "Your mother did not tell you?"

"No."

Her face was a study. "I do not understand," she said.

"And nor do I. Except that my mother wanted me to be my stepfather's child. She was foolish about that. Blind. Obsessive. Howard and I loved her so much that we tried to go along with this. I certainly could have loved him had I not known, even as a small child, that he did not love me. Small children are much more aware than grown-ups recognise."

"Indeed," she said, looking appalled.

"When I was told the truth about my parentage I reckoned he was resentful at having been stuck with me. When my mother died he simply turned his back."

"But he gave you Andrew's address?"

"No. He was devastated by her death. Knocked sideways. We both were. I think he wasn't quite himself. His grief took the form of turning openly against me. Maybe he allowed himself to see that he could perhaps have had more of Margaret had I not been there for her. I don't know. She did spend a great deal of energy trying to bring us together." I stared out to sea, remembering. "A kind of insanity comes over people in shock, sometimes, I think."

"I know." She spoke in scarcely more than a whisper and I guessed she was talking about the son who had died.

"Howard had letters he had found after my mother's death. Your address was on them. I suppose he felt duty-bound to give them to me, but it seems he couldn't bring himself to do it until I went to him – this week, only this week – to tell him I had discovered my father was Ben Tyrill." I didn't say he had given me the letters in a mood of spite.

"And yet he loved your mother? This I do not understand."

I told her he had married again. She looked shocked. "Not because he has forgotten Margaret. I think he was still grieving and needed comfort." I didn't tell her about the money, either. There was no point. Besides, I did owe him some gratitude. He had produced the letters.

"Andrew will be glad," she said, "that it wasn't your fault you didn't come. And so am I."

We sat in silence for a while, looking at the little waves lapping at the sand. "Would you like to tell me about the boy who was killed?" I asked tentatively.

"Andrew was beginning to forget." Her voice was surface calm, but I sensed emotion in the shape of her words, the deeper tone. "The success of these Ben Tyrill books has given him such great pleasure, and renewed confidence. There was a great change in him. Part of the forgetting was sending Leslie to his old school in England. I didn't want him to go, but I knew it was part of Andrew's learning to live with the past, so I didn't protest. Then there was the plane crash. He was flying home for the holidays. Andrew went into his shell again." She paused. Folded her hands in her lap. "He thought, in a superstitious way, he was being told he had to stay out of England. And then the Raphael publicity came up and the papers started saying as it came from this area it could be one of Andrew Hollis's fakes. That after twenty-six years he had grown brave again."

I desperately wanted to ask if it was he who had offered the picture for sale. I did not dare.

"This picture was offered to the National Gallery in London by a Dutch agent who would not disclose the name of his client. Then someone came forward to say he knew this particular painting belonged to a Bolivian millionaire, and that the Bolivian had said he would never part with it. He suggested the agent might consider the possibility that he had a fake. Someone found out the seller was not the Bolivian, but a man who lived south of Rome. They are saying openly that Andrew Hollis, who was involved in an art swindle twenty-years ago, lives south of Rome."

"Why can't the Bolivian have the fake?" I asked.

Donna looked thoughtful. "I suppose they have considered that. I suppose they would make tests if there was any doubt. But whatever happens, the publicity could not have come at a worse time, when Andrew's most ambitious work was starting to be talked about in England. He thought, after all those years, that the old case would be forgotten. He used his own name on this book.

"You can imagine what happened," Donna went on, "as soon as it became known Ben Tyrill was Andrew Hollis, with the news about the picture breaking at the same time. Suddenly, we were besieged with reporters. He feels he is back where he was twenty-six years ago." Donna was silent, looking sadly out on the sparkling bay.

"What has this to do with me?" I asked. "You started to say he did not write to me when Mother died because—" I broke off, remembering she had not told my father about yesterday's visit. "Why does he not want to see me?"

She looked up, her big dark eyes eloquent and sad. "You are part of England," she said. "No more than that. His son died because he sent him to an English school. His countrymen treated him badly, and your mother . . . Now, it is English reporters who are after him, trying to pin this new forgery on him. Perhaps he feels this repetition – perhaps he feels—" She stopped.

"Go on," I said, speaking gently because I could see she was distressed.

Donna threw her hands out in a gesture of helplessness. "He has no reason to think our marriage could go wrong, but I think your arrival will disturb him greatly. Too much of the past is coming up at once, and he seems to have lost confidence. I have been trying to find the best way of telling him you are here."

"Perhaps he won't care to meet me anyway," I said bleakly, realising how high the cards were stacked against me. "He never tried to see me."

"It was for your own good, Jane. He really believed that. Forgive me for saying this, because you are probably fond of your stepfather, but your father did not admire him over-much, and he felt you would have a happier time if your mother's husband thought of you as his own. Andrew thought visits from him would build up a barrier between you and Mr Knight."

"Did you agree?" I asked.

"No, I did not agree. A child to me is—" she shrugged "—a child, always." She gave me a wry look. "But, as he explained, he left before you were born. He said one could not *leave* a child one had never met."

That was logical, I had to agree, though the logic did not lessen the hurt. Above us, a sudden gust of warm wind ran through the shrubs, bringing with it the dry dust of the hillside and scent of pines and oleander. "What am I to do, then?" I asked this new stepmother.

She did not pause to work it out. Everything seemed very clear in Donna's mind. She took my hand, holding it so gently in hers that a lump came to my throat. She said, "Come back this evening, about five o'clock. I will talk to him now. He needs his children, and perhaps – who knows – perhaps you can help take the place of Leslie. Leslie, my little English boy," Donna ended sadly, then added, "Where are you staying?"

I told her. And, "Yes, I will come back," I said.

Bertini had fallen asleep in the sun, his big dark head lolling on his shoulder. She spoke to him in Italian. He woke up, stretched, yawned lazily and pulled the boat in. Donna was still waving as we sped across the bay. I waved back, warmed by her friendliness and unable to believe my good fortune.

I lunched alone, with one eye on the entrance to the cloisters, waiting for Carl to come and knowing full well it was better that he should not. Then I went to my room and settled down to read in a deck chair on my little balcony, waiting for five o'clock. The afternoon sky was leaden, the horizon merging into it, the water still. It was a foreign sky to me, and I could not tell whether it presaged a thunderstorm or a run of boiling days. The latter, I hoped. I opened my paperback, reading half pages without comprehension, glancing at my watch, and glancing back again in case I had made a mistake and it was, in fact, later than I thought. At last, finding the tension unendurable, I decided to walk down into the town to fill in time until I could go to the Villa Passerina.

I went to the wardrobe and selected a dress with care: a blue cotton, sleeveless and plain. I brushed my hair carefully. It seemed shades lighter since this morning's sun. I stood back from the looking glass, inspecting myself critically. Donna had said my father had wanted his son to be English. Perhaps he would see something he liked, then, in me.

My nerves were so tightly strung that I jumped when the telephone shrilled.

"*Signorina*, there is a gentleman downstairs to see you."

"Mr Beaumont?"

"No, *signorina*. He is Mr Hollis."

Chapter Five

The afternoon sun was high, bathing the cloisters in bright Mediterranean light. At the side, half in the shadows, stood a tall, spare man with fair, greying hair swept back from a high forehead. He wore a short-sleeved jumper in that deep shade of blue that was so prevalent in Italy, and grey, English-looking trousers. He was facing the small arch at the entrance to the stairs and as I appeared our eyes held. I smiled nervously. His own smile was warm, but equally uncertain. He came towards me, picking his way between the tables. He held out both hands.

"Jane."

It was a moment charged with emotion. He said, "Come over here and sit down." He did not attempt to embrace me. We sat on either side of one of the little square tables. "Well, my daughter?" said Andrew. Then suddenly he smiled, properly. "You look like me," he said.

"Yes." We sat there smiling at each other, both out of our depth, I think. I had the feeling he was thrown off balance by seeing the family resemblance.

He said, "I have got to get used to this. I never allowed myself to think of you as my daughter. I always thought of you as belonging to Howard."

"You did think of me sometimes?" I tried to sound casual, as though I was merely making polite conversation.

He was looking at me, hard, as though he had to memorise my features. I wondered if he was as full of suppressed emotion as I and that was why he didn't answer immediately. Or was he wondering what to say so that my feelings would not be hurt? He signed to the waiter. "This calls for a drink," he said. "What would you like, my dear?"

"*Una Campari, per favore*," I said.

He looked startled.

"No, I don't speak Italian. I learned that today."

He laughed, looking pleased, as though I had complimented him. The waiter came and stood before us. My father ordered two Camparis. He leaned towards me, placing his forearms on the table, looking into my eyes. "Sometimes?" He repeated my word with sadness. "Oh yes, I thought of you." He paused, still looking at me. "Howard and Margaret's daughter," he said, enunciating slowly and carefully, as one might repeat a well-known phrase, "for that is how we had decided it should be. Tell me about yourself," he said.

"I want to know why you opted out of my life," I replied, thinking, you can't disappear out of a child's life, then one afternoon, between lunch and tea, ask her to lay it out before you like a map so that you had missed nothing, after all. My feelings of resentment were the scars I bore. I couldn't lock his sins of omission in a box and throw away the key.

He looked taken aback at my question. He took his time about answering. "I was the product of a broken home," he said. "I was shunted between my mother and father and grandparents. Aunts, even. And always they produced the failings of the other parent and laid them before me. I found it disturbing. A child has a natural sense of loyalty.

"And my parents had filled my absences in their lives with matters that couldn't be put aside when it came to their turn to take me over. I was very aware of not belonging in either camp. And aware that their lives were complete in a different way when I wasn't there. I didn't want that to happen to you."

And it wouldn't have. I thought of his warmhearted wife who would have made me so very, very welcome. Then it occurred to me that he probably hadn't remarried for another ten years or more. Marisa was fourteen years younger than me. He might have found it impossible to look after a small child. Yes, I might well have ended up with his relatives.

"Were you happy?" he asked.

Even recognising his problems, I didn't want him to get off scott free. "Howard was Mother's husband," I said. "He was never my father."

The waiter came and put the drinks down, geranium-coloured

like the plants in the stone tubs on the terrace. He stared down into his Campari. "I'm sorry."

"Howard is very respectable, you know. He must have hated marrying a pregnant woman. I found their marriage certificate. It was dated one month before I was born. I was just about old enough to know what that meant. Mother laughed, but Howard was angry. He told me then that I wasn't his child and suggested that I call him by his Christian name." I had had my revenge and felt the better for it. Better still when I saw the horrified expression in my father's eyes.

"My poor child," he said. And then again, "My poor child. We went to no end of trouble, pulling strings, to get the divorce through before you were born, so that you could be his." He reached to touch my hand, then withdrew, as though pre-empting me, and changed the subject.

"What happened to Margaret? As the result of an accident, the announcement in the paper said."

I told him.

"How dreadful! And she was still young."

"Forty-five. And pretty, still."

He smiled at that. "When you're forty-five you may find you expect to be pretty still." He sat back in his chair, looking directly at me. "I didn't want to say this, but perhaps I should. You know your mother. It won't surprise you that she couldn't make up her mind between Howard and me. I was away a lot, buying pictures. Howard was always there. Always," he said, gazing into the bougainvillaea, remembering. I could see the memory in the hard lines that appeared between his nose and chin. "Of course, Margaret was lonely." He added, "She was very young."

I closed my eyes, tortured by the unreason of his tolerance. What my sweet mother had needed, and what she would have responded to, I felt certain, was a harsh demand, a threat, a slap, even. She would have known where she was, then. But all the same, it seemed she loved them both and, I guessed, Howard was the stronger man as well as being the man who was around. With that understanding, my resentment began to fade. I was looking at other people's lives. I had no right to judge. "Have you ever had regrets?" I asked.

"Until I remarried. Yes, my dear, of course. And has your life been happy? Apart from—" He gestured, dismissing that which we had discussed.

"Yes." I looked up at him. "But I used to think about you a lot. I suppose I romanticised you. The unknown is invariably glamorous."

He smiled then, a gentle, understanding smile. "And now?"

"You're rather what I expected, really. A tall, lean man, going grey. You had to be like me, because I was not at all like Mother."

He raised his glass and indicated that I raise mine. "I would like you to come and stay. Let's drink to happy relations, from now on."

"Happy relations," I said. Suddenly, I was aware of another presence close at hand, and turned. Carl was standing less than a yard away, looking down at us, his eyes bright, friendly.

"Is it all right?" he asked.

I jumped up. My heart began to beat faster and I felt my colour rise. "Yes, it is all right." Andrew looked up in surprise, pushed his chair back and rose, his manner faintly wary.

Before I had a chance to do so, Carl introduced himself. "We met on the train," he said. "My mother lives in Salerno. I was able to give Jane a ride."

"That was very kind of you," Andrew said courteously. They shook hands. He turned to me. "What size is your bag?"

"Not very big. Would you like to walk?"

Carl interposed. "If you could do with a car, I'd be only too happy to help. Jane's bag isn't that big, as she said, but you wouldn't want to walk up a hill with it."

I noted that he had said 'a hill' not 'the hill'. He was smart, all right. Even so, the wary look came back into Andrew's face. Carl saw it, too. He said, sounding tremendously casual, certainly not justifying his presence and his car, "My mother met the train with her car yesterday. I haven't taken it back yet."

It was the moment for me to say, "He is a reporter." I would have said it, if I had not been already more than half in love with him. I should have said it anyway; mentioning his mother was a deliberate effort to deceive. Andrew was taken in. I wrestled with my conscience. If I spoke I might never see Carl again. If I did not, he would, inevitably, drive a stake between my father and me. But I felt, even at this early stage, as one always feels about a relative whom one loves, or in this case, wishes to love, that he would be innocent. And a newspaper can do no harm to an innocent man.

I had been very alone for a long time. I wanted to have my cake and eat it. I had wondered how Carl dared to leave me yesterday. Now I knew. There are some people who by their very confidence in themselves seem to manipulate fate. "Shall we take him up on his offer?" I smiled up into my father's blue English eyes.

"Yes. Yes," he said to Carl. "It's very kind of you."

We drove up through the town to the Villa Passerina and paused outside while my father, leaning across Carl, sounded the horn three times. A small, dark boy ran out from behind some ornamental brickwork that partially concealed a wrought-iron gate, and unlocked the garage doors. This was Nino, their housekeeper's son, Andrew said. We left him to lock the gate again and to bring the bag. Andrew led us down the steps behind the garage and into the garden, then down the lower steps where I had been before when I climbed over the gate and was thrown out by Maria; onto the terrace at the back of the house. Carl was following in silence. In my excitement, I scarcely thought of him. Or perhaps some part of me dared not.

Maria saw us first, and gave a great joyous cry that brought Donna running.

She came with hands outstretched and took mine. "I am so glad, so very glad." She turned to Andrew, patted one cheek and kissed the other. "Now you will be happier, my darling." She was full of warmth and certainty. I glanced up at my father's face and saw he was smiling.

"This is Carl," I said.

"Carl?" She looked at him uncertainly, holding out a hand with equal hesitation. I sensed she knew, or thought she knew, who he was.

"It is an English custom to dispense with surnames," he said, smiling. Carl Beaumont."

"Ah yes," said Donna. "I have not had the pleasure of meeting you. You are a friend of—"

"Yes." His intervention was unhurried, quite natural. "I know your husband's publishers."

"I met him on the train," I said. "He has been very kind to me. He had his car at the hotel, so he brought my things up."

"We will give him a drink," said Andrew genially, and turning to Carl: "Did you say you know my publishers?"

"I know the Lambardinis. Yes."

Donna led us across the tiled hall and onto the balcony. There were prettily cushioned cane chairs, a glass-topped table made of wrought-iron and some straight-backed seats to match. The view was magnificent. The whole bay, not as I saw it in part from my hotel room. We were looking across the town from the opposite direction.

"You speak very good English," I said to my new step-mother.

"I taught for a year in Reading. Do you know Reading, by the Thames? A nice place, and full of nice English boys. I had a lot of fun. But I was very cold. I was glad, in the end, to get back to Rome. But," she linked an arm through Andrew's, "it gave me a taste for Englishmen, as you will see."

She was good for him, this laughing Italian wife. I could see he was a serious man, but he brightened in her presence. Her affectionate, teasing laughter, I felt sure, must have helped him to forget the past.

Andrew said, "What would you like to drink, Carl?" and turned towards a door that led to an inner room, a study, or library, perhaps.

"Shall I come with you and help?" He followed closely at Andrew's heels, friendly, cooperative, but with that immensely alert air he sometimes assumed.

I followed them across the threshold into a panelled room with bookshelves and a desk. There were half a dozen very beautiful pictures on the walls, and a small bronze statue on a tall table in a corner. The pictures were set in gilt frames and carefully lit from small bracket lights. My first reaction was one of astonishment, because the pictures all looked familiar. Then I recognised one – *La Gioconda*. I had seen that in the Louvre during one of my educational sorties to Paris with my class from school. I gave an involuntary exclamation of surprise. "*The Gioconda Smile*!"

Andrew turned to look at it, smiling deprecatingly. "Perhaps you don't know that I am an artist of sorts. I spent three weeks in the Louvre doing that copy. I am quite proud of it. Do you know anything about art?"

I could not reply. My throat was constricted. I threw a panicky look at Carl and saw his eyes glaze over. He moved from one picture to the next. There was one of Charles II, in his long, black wig, and one copied from a Gauguin, one of his Pacific Island paintings. You couldn't mistake them.

Andrew said, pointing, "Do you like that one? *Mountains in Provence*. I did it from a print. I have never actually seen Cézanne's original. It's in the National Gallery. I have had a great deal of pleasure from that picture. If one cannot afford the real thing – and I can't – the next best is to have a good copy. You know, I suppose," he addressed Carl, "that I once had an art gallery of my own?"

I could not look at Carl now. I did not dare. Andrew had taken some glasses from a cupboard and was saying, "We didn't decide, did we? What are you going to drink?"

"Campari again, please," I managed to say. Carl completed a quick inspection of the room, then turned towards Andrew, hands in his pockets, his face a study. "I'll have that, too. You are a very good artist, sir."

"No, no," Andrew replied. "Just a hack. I can reproduce. I've never done anything worthwhile in an original. I know a lot about restoration, but I prefer to write. I paint merely for my own pleasure. I have done over a hundred reproductions of my favourite old masters, but I can't have them all on the walls. I swap them over periodically."

We went back to the balcony with our drinks in our hands, and Andrew brought one for Donna. She was lying back on a brightly cushioned seat, smiling and looking very pleased with life. I scarcely remember the rest of that social half-hour before Carl left. I only recall that when he did make his excuses I went to the door with him, grasped him convulsively by the hand, looked up into his face and found myself unable to word the entreaty in my heart for fear of making the situation worse. In the end I said, "I want to see you alone. Can you meet me later?"

"Sure," he said easily. His face was grave.

"At the trattoria? About six?" I was thinking that I could perhaps slip away before dinner.

He nodded. "I'll be there."

"You won't go anywhere? You won't leave?"

He merely shrugged. I stood watching him go up the steps with dread. When I went back inside Andrew and Donna were talking. I heard her say, ". . . I think we both met him at the Lambardinis'. He is to marry Evelina Lambardini, is he not?"

I stood quite still in the tiled hall, wanting to die.

The children came home from school. They ran noisily through the hall, shouting a greeting to Maria, who opened the door to them. Marisa came direct to the balcony looking for her parents, saw me and blinked in astonishment. Andrew said, "You have met Jane, I believe." I waited for him to tell them I was their sister, but he only added, looking beyond Marisa to the other two, "She is coming to stay with us for a while."

Marisa looked pleased and Lucia announced delightedly, "She will make Enrico take us out in the boat again." Both girls were quaintly dressed in the white pinafores all the children wore to school. Marisa was too tall and leggy for hers, but Lucia looked adorable. Guido acknowledged my presence with a rough little bow, then bounded energetically out of the room. The others followed him.

Donna said, "I will show you to your room. We will tell the children about you later."

"These are Andrew's pictures," she said with pride as we went down the marble stairs. On either side hung half a dozen portraits, some of which were frighteningly familiar to me.

There was Franz Hals' *Laughing Cavalier* and Vincent Van Gogh's famous chair.

"Why does he do it?" I asked, my nervousness showing in my voice and no doubt in my face. "Why does he do copies, when – when—" I made a gesture of helplessness.

"He loves the old masters," Donna said placidly. "He does not count himself imaginative. He says there are enough second-rate artists filling the galleries now, without his adding to them. He has some Original Hollises, as he calls them" – Donna's eyes twinkled – "and I like them, but he considers them poor. Perhaps he will show them to you some time. But these," she turned and looked up from the hall below, indicating the paintings on the walls above us, "these give him immense pleasure."

"Presumably," I said, "he could earn his living making copies. People pay quite high prices for copies, I believe."

Donna was opening the door of my room. "Ah yes, of course. But he would not. Not after that other affair. You see," she added with a candour that frightened me, "he does them far too well."

"You mean," I asked bleakly, "if he really wanted to add a signature . . ." I could not go on, and anyway, Donna evidently did not wish to reply because she shrugged and changed the subject.

"What he would really like to do is start his own gallery again. He loves to be with beautiful things. Perhaps he will one day. Although with this business coming up again, after all these years, his confidence has taken a knock. This is your room, my dear."

There was a lace-covered bed, a small, antique dressing-table, and a narrow, elegant sofa.

"How pretty!" I exclaimed, my apprehension sliding away in sudden delight. I went to the window.

The villa clung to the cliff, one room deep. I was looking out on shrubs and cacti. I could have leaned through the window and touched them with my hand. I was on the ground floor, if it could be described that way, the bedrooms on this level being in the lowest section of the house. From here the garden rolled away towards the sea. The steps leading down to the water ran off the path outside.

Donna came to stand beside me and put an affectionate arm round my waist. I turned to smile at her, deeply moved. Nothing must go wrong, I thought. Nothing. I won't let anything happen to this.

"I will leave you to wander round the garden if you wish. I shall be busy for a while," Donna said. "You will hear the bell. It sounds grand to ring a dinner bell, but the house and garden are so full of stairs, it is the only way to avoid wearing ourselves out."

When she had gone I glanced at my watch. It was nearly six o'clock. If I were to see Carl at the trattoria I must hurry. I put a leg over the windowsill, slid out onto the path, sped up the steps and, hoping I would not be seen from some window and be thought to be running away, dashed for the gate.

He was there, sitting at the same little table where we had had breakfast. He glanced up as I came in. I sat down opposite him, my arms on the table. He looked grave.

"Well?" he said.

"Well?" I returned bleakly. "You came here for a story. What are you going to do?"

"I suppose I have to do my job," he said.

"And a pretty sneaky job it is—" I whispered angrily. My voice broke because I was thinking that he had kissed me knowing he was going to marry Evelina Lambardini. "You kissed me because you wanted an introduction to my father," I said. "You got to the villa under false pretences. You've got no conscience!"

Carl took one of my hands in a firm grip. "I have a great deal of conscience," he said. "I have a responsibility to the people who employ me to do my work properly. Listen, Jane, your father is probably a forger. You've got to face facts. All those pictures—"

"If he were a forger," I broke in angrily, "he would be an incredible fool to have all those pictures on show. He would hide them away in an attic and pretend he didn't paint at all." I jerked my hand away.

"I think you have hit the nail on the head," he replied gravely. "I think he is an incredible fool. I think he is naïve. Lots of clever men are. They're so concerned with what they're doing they forget about the harsh world outside."

I felt distraught. At last, when I had calmed a little, I said, "What are you going to do about it? Are you going to report it all to your news service?"

"I've no proof," he said.

A waiter came and stood over us. "*Cafè, signore*?" Carl nodded and the man went away.

"This Bolivian who is kicking up the fuss contacted my employers. He wants us to find out who is selling that picture. I was put on your father's trail because I know the area. They thought I might not only get on to your father, but I might also be able to find out where he got the original from. Now, let's not play games, Jane. Although the sort of proof we have is useless, the picture obviously came from Andrew. If you believe him to be innocent, why don't you ask?"

"How can I ask?" I whispered.

"No, of course."

The waiter came with two cups of black coffee. I said, "I may as well go back. There is nothing more to be said, I suppose." Then a thought flashed into my mind. "Why don't you go to the Dutch agent who is handling this wretched picture? Why don't you question him?"

"What's the point? He is offering it as an original. I would rather track down the man who showed the picture to your father."

"Why?"

"It completes the story, doesn't it? Did the Bolivian loan his picture to Andrew to make a copy?"

"What?"

He grinned. "There's an awful lot of jiggery-pokery in the world, Jane."

"Well, I've no doubt you'll get what you want," I said, my misery turning to bitterness. "You've been trained to get things out of people. You did a remarkably good job on me."

He reached out with both hands and before I could draw mine back, had grasped them. My heart turned over. I sat there feeling warm and foolish and angry and frightened, while the words I should be saying to him danced through my mind: *You're going to marry Evelina!* And he was going to be ruthless with a man who was too gentle, too naïve, perhaps, to recognise him for what he was.

"You had better get yourself used to the idea," Carl said gently, "that your father is in for trouble. There is nothing either you or I can do about it. Even if I pulled out, it wouldn't make any difference in the long run. My employers would put another chap on the job."

"I shall have to tell him you are a reporter." I tried to drag my hands away. "Let me go. Please let me go." I wanted to say: *This is your fault. You are going to ruin everything. You are going to come between my father and me.* But I could not say it because I was the guilty one. It was my fault, and mine alone that Carl had seen the paintings at the Villa Passerina.

Marisa was quiet over dinner, watching me, but saying little. I wondered, with a touch of unease, why Donna had said they would tell the children later. Was Andrew leaving the way clear to send me home if I, his English daughter, should add to his bad luck?

After dinner, Andrew took me to his library with its big walnut desk and floor to ceiling bookshelves, his row of beautiful Ben Tyrill volumes that had made him famous, with their cleverly designed jackets and big colour plates. Donna tactfully left us alone, making a show of being busy with the children. It was my opportunity to tell him I had introduced a journalist to his home; to prepare him for the fact that the new daughter he had welcomed, against his better judgement, had already let him down. I looked up at him and tried to find a way to say it, but I couldn't. If he had really accepted me, if he had told the children who I was, I think I could have confessed, but when one is standing on a precipice one does not give oneself a push. I will think about it tomorrow, I told myself. Tomorrow . . .

"Where do you do your painting?" I asked. "Have you a studio somewhere?"

"My studio is here," Andrew replied. "Would you like to see it?"

I said I would. He took a key from the top drawer in his desk and led me into the hall. "We have to go outside. It is a garden room, or basement, opening onto the terrace below the bedrooms. Come."

We went down the stairs past the extraordinary, baffling pictures, along the bedroom passage then out of the side door I might have taken instead of slipping out via my bedroom window.

We followed a narrow, curving path lit by two lights set against the exterior of the villa. Then we stepped onto a narrow terrace partially enclosed by trees. Andrew inserted his key in a door set in the wall.

I had never seen an artist's studio before. There were several easels leaning against a wall and one standing upright. There was a palette daubed with a multitude of colours, a stack of canvases against a wall, a narrow table strewn with papers, and an enormous cupboard with the door slightly ajar.

"It's neither tidy nor interesting," he said ruefully, rubbing his chin. "I don't allow Maria in. She would be shocked. Donna has a tidy up now and again."

"May I see your paintings?" I asked. "Some of the original ones?"

He smiled. "I told you, my dear, I am not very proud of them."

"I am no judge of art. Do let me see."

He went over to the stack that leaned against the wall, bent down and selected one. "This you may recognise," he said, then added drily, "An original Hollis-Constable. It was done from memory. A scene near East Bergholt."

The picture was, to my untutored eyes, very well done, and certainly there were strong Constable overtones. "Why?" I asked. "Why have you not tried to develop a style of your own?"

"I have already told you, it's not in me," he said. "My writing is original, but my painting is not."

"May I see the others?"

He shrugged. "If you want to." But he did not stand back and let me go through them.

He picked one out here and there, turned others over quickly. I couldn't tell whether it was impatience with his work or impatience with me for wanting to see it. Or if there was work here he did not wish me to see. I could have said, *Why can't I look at all of them?* and might have done so if Carl had not been on my mind. I was already on a tight-rope, recognising the need to step very, very carefully.

He brought out three or four still lifes. I liked them. "Never mind that I know nothing about art," I said. "They're very pleasing."

He stood looking at me, holding another canvas between finger and thumb. "I'm surprised you didn't have some sort of art training," he said. "There's so much satisfaction in it."

"I really haven't the talent."

He looked whimsical. "You mean, your talent hasn't been discovered. But it's latent in everyone. You can be taught to draw and paint."

"It somehow didn't come my way." I thought he ought to be able to guess, as I now did, why art was not discussed in our household. "I like doing physiotherapy," I said lamely then seeing he was disappointed in my answer, added, "I shall be very interested from now on. Very." It occurred to me that my friend Rosie, who sent me on this quest for my father, was very much a part of the art world. Odd, that. And yet, not really. I suppose one doesn't talk about one's work if friends don't show any interest. Perhaps she might have invited me to some of her glamorous parties where I would have met artists, if she thought I would care to go.

"What did you have on the walls when you were growing up?" he asked. He was very intent now. I could see he really wanted to know.

I cast my mind back to that neat house in Highgate where Carol, the new wife, lived with my stepfather now. I had thought it a little insensitive of her to move into another woman's home, but for all I knew Howard might have tried to sell. The market had been depressed for years. "There were a good many mirrors on the walls," I said. "A few prints. My mother loved antiques. You will know that."

He nodded.

"She had some very good pieces."

"So, you're interested in antiques?"

He hadn't missed the point, after all. "That's the way it works," I said, keeping my voice light. "But I can't afford to buy them."

"You didn't get any of hers?"

I shook my head.

He said, "I'm sorry. You've had a bad deal."

I had an urge to say he could have prevented that bad deal but I was afraid to speak out now. Carl, by following me here, had tied my hands. I had had my say the day we met at the Maria Convento. I was going to have to be content with that.

He showed me one or two more paintings. I liked them all. We talked a little. I wished I could be as much at ease with him as I was with Donna. But then, I held no resentment towards her, and my conscience was clear. After a while we wandered back to the house. It was dark in the garden. Very dark indeed beneath the lemon trees. I sniffed at the scented Mediterranean air. "This is a lovely place," I said. "So tranquil."

"I hope you'll stay a long time. What about your work?"

"Someone has taken my place. But of course I can't leave her there too long in case she takes root. Besides, I have to pay the mortgage. It's rather vast." I had never asked myself why I needed that expensive flat. Now, suddenly I knew. It was my safe anchorage. I would have been happy in a bedsit, spending my money on visits to Italy, if things had worked out that way.

"I'm sure we could manage something there," he said.

I said, "I'm a big girl now. Thanks all the same." I was glad he had offered, though.

Later, I went slowly down the stairs to my bedroom, examining the pictures one by one, my feet lingering on each marble step. They frightened me, these copies that Andrew had painted. I was baffled by the simulated age cracks, the antique look. My mind ran back, inevitably, to that evening when my stepfather had told me Andrew and his partner in their London gallery had been accused of selling forged old masters. Painting and selling them? I had to consider now, it might be true.

Chapter Six

I wakened before the sun was up. I got up and went to the window. Outside, the sky was lightening, and across a limpid bay I could hear the cries of fishermen. I could see them now, a fleet of tiny boats in the bright moonlight, making their way to port. On an impulse, I pulled on a pair of jeans and jumper, thrust my feet into sandals, ran a comb through my hair and crept quietly out and up the stairs. The front door was locked and bolted. I opened it as gently as I could, wincing at the inevitable scraping and groaning of iron on iron, and slipped out into the garden. It was night-silent here, but far in the distance I could still hear the fishermen's cries. I unlocked the gate and set off alone down the road to the beach.

I think I shall never forget that morning. I sat on the sea wall watching the sun coming up over the mountains and the moon going down into the sea. I watched the sea change from pale silver to grey, then green, and lose its limpid look to a freshening breeze. I listened to a fisherman singing, his voice rising mellow, golden and clear, and I watched the brown skinned fisherfolk come ashore carrying their great basketware trays of fish.

And then to complete the magic, when I was thinking of returning to the villa, from the direction of the Hotel Maria Convento a tall man in a towelling robe came striding along the sands. My heart turned a silly flip and I smiled, though he was still too far away to see my face, even had he been looking my way. He walked to the middle of the beach, threw his robe down and ran into the water. I sat there watching as he swam with a fast crawl straight out into the bay. The fishermen had gone now and he had the morning to himself. He stopped about a hundred and fifty yards out, dived, flung himself on his back and floated, then dived again. When he rosc it seemed as though he was looking in my direction, so I waved and he, recognising me, waved back, then swam slowly inshore.

I was waiting for him with his robe over my arm. He ran up the sand, a little breathless and shaking the water out of his hair. "Well, hello, early riser!"

"Hello. So you are an early riser, too! I never expected to see you in the water at six o'clock in the morning. There is some spartan in you, after all."

"There is, indeed. B-r-r, the sun's not high enough. Are you going to run with me?"

"Why not?" He took my hand and we ran together the length of the beach, slipping and sliding on the cold, damp sand. I was breathless when we came to the steps that led on to the promenade.

"You're out of condition," he said reprovingly.

"I'm not, you know," I retorted with some spirit. "No one can run on sand. Maybe you, but no one else." We laughed together and he pulled me up the steps.

"You must meet me down here for a swim tomorrow morning. Swimming is a very social exercise. I never enjoy it fully, alone. And, of course, it's the best part of the day."

"I'll come." I promised impulsively, forgetting it was not my habit to waken so early.

"Do you think your family would mind if you came to dinner with me tomorrow evening?" he asked as we walked along the front.

"They might be glad to get rid of me, if by then they've found out you're a journalist," I said.

He ignored that. "I want to take you to my mother's."

I stopped dead. "What?"

"Why so surprised?"

I glared up at him, or tried to glare, but my eyes were misty and sad. "I may as well tell you I overheard Donna telling Andrew that you're engaged to Evelina Lambardini." I hated saying it out loud. Making it real.

"What a thing to say before breakfast." He gripped the hand nearest to him, squeezed it and, leaning down, kissed me on the cheek.

"What a thing to do before breakfast," I said childishly. I was hurt at his duplicity.

"You take life too seriously, Jane. It's serious enough in itself."

He was right of course, in a way. But, "Look here," I said, "I'm in a serious position because of you. How can you expect me to laugh about it? And how can you take me to dine with your mother when you know very well I won't be welcome?"

"My mother always welcomes my friends."

"Oh," I exploded, "you're full of tricks." I couldn't understand why he was blatantly trying to make me fall in love with him, wanting to inflict me on his mother, yet unwilling to deny that he was to marry Evelina. Maybe he played like this with every woman he met, making fools of them. "I'm sorry," I said swiftly, "but I can't go to your mother's. Not unless I get thrown out, in which case I shall no doubt be glad of a meal, but not at your mother's place. I want to make that clear. Not at your mother's place," I repeated.

"If you get thrown out you'll still have me," he said.

"You and Evelina Lambardini," I retorted and snatched my hand away. "You had better go and change before you freeze. And I must go back and have breakfast." Wild horses were not going to drag me out with him tomorrow night.

I came to know my father's family that day. We all went down to the lido to swim and watch Guido with his new canoe. Graciously, he allowed me to ride in it when Lucia, the little one, could be persuaded to get out. Lucia was a constant worry to her mother because, although she could not swim, she had no fear of the water. About midday Guido decided to take his canoe off. "I want to go round to the cave."

"Why, Guido?" his mother asked.

"Alessandro and Cesare are coming to play smugglers this afternoon, and I promised I would leave the canoe there ready."

"Ah! I see!" Donna, it seemed, understood little boys very well. "Come, Lucia *cara*!" She held out her arms. "We will go round the cliff to the cave and walk back with Guido."

But Lucia was not to be moved. She gripped the canoe sides, announcing defiantly, "I am going with Guido."

And, in the end, she did.

Donna and I went back up the steps to the villa and then up beside it until we reached the back of the building where the path ran parallel and just below the road. Donna had said there was no track from the lido across to Guido's cave for the ground was steep and rocky, broken here and there by straight drops where the water had worn the hillside away. We left the garden by a tiny gate that led to a cliff path running between the neighbouring villas and the road. I could see Donna was anxious, as well she might be, but she hid it admirably as we hurried over the stony little path towards the point. "All of my children are individuals," she said. "It's a running battle to keep them safe."

The path was rough and narrow and the dry brush that grew across our way scratched my bare legs. "Nobody comes along this path," Donna told me. "It runs in the same direction as the road, so there is no point in using it. But the traffic is a constant worry, and the children are safe here. Also, they like it. It's something of a secret path for them."

Below us now, we could see the children. Guido had nosed the canoe in towards the cliff and Lucia was waving. We waved back and hurried on down the rock-strewn, partially-stepped cliff path.

"Are you going to tell the children I am their half-sister?" I asked tentatively.

"Of course. Of course. We will tell them now," she returned.

"And Andrew? Does he want them to know?"

Donna shrugged smilingly. "Well, of course, Andrew rules the house," she said, her dark eyes twinkling. "A man has to be king in his own home, but life would be very static if we waited for the kings to move, would it not, Jane?"

"You're very sweet, Donna, and I hope my father realises how lucky he is to have you."

"Oh yes," she replied. "He realises that. We are very happy with each other."

"I'm glad," I said. So both of my parents had found happiness. That was a plus.

We slithered on down the track. There were some dangerous-looking cactus plants growing in the dry grass on either side. Considering Donna had said she was not agile I was surprised how well she managed. I was already thinking it was going to be a long haul back. We came at last to the foot of the cliff. Here we had to scramble over some boulders for there was no path. Beyond the rocks the sea water lapped against a small strip of sand. We could see Guido and Lucia in their canoe now, paddling towards the entrance to the cave. Lucia waved. We picked our way across some shale and came on to a flattish shelf of sea grass that ran to within twenty feet of the mouth of the grotto. Cave, they had called it. It looked like a grotto to me. It was enormous. A great arch-shaped gap in the cliff. Guido brought the canoe in until its nose struck the bank.

"Now you can get out," Guido said.

Lucia protested, "I want to go into the cave."

"No, *cara mia*, you cannot do that," Donna said. "Come on, jump out as Guido says."

"Why can't I go with him?" The little girl was close to tears.

"She probably could," said Guido, looking at his sister with head on one side, considering.

"No, dear. I wouldn't like to trust Lucia not to overbalance on that narrow ledge as she comes out. When you can swim you shall go in," Donna said. She turned to me. "The water isn't deep inside, but certainly well over Lucia's head."

"Shall I go with them?" I was intrigued. Anxious to see what was inside this great, gaping hole in the cliff. "I'm not very heavy. And I'm a good swimmer. I'll look after Lucia and rescue her if she falls in."

"Yes! Yes!" shrieked the child.

"Now that solves the problem. Jane will go with you, *cara mia*."

I took off my shoes, stepped down on the rocks and climbed aboard. It was a child's canoe. I wasn't certain it was going to float with my weight added to that of the two children. It sank a little lower in the water. We whooped with dismay, waiting for it to settle. It did. Donna removed her sandals, found a foothold in the rocks and pushed us out. I put my arms round Lucia and held her firmly between my knees in case she should disturb the canoe's balance.

Guido swung it round and paddled towards the entrance, grumbling about my weight. "You're heavy, Jane."

I apologised. "I could take over the paddling but you might end up in Timbuktu. I've never paddled a canoe before."

Lucia was intrigued. "Where's Timbuktu?" and without waiting for a reply, "Let's go there."

"Next week," I said, humouring her.

"There's the ledge you come out on," said Guido, pointing as we entered the grotto. "It's wide enough."

It was indeed about a foot in width. "I'm sure Lucia will manage that," I said, "and if not we'll swim. I'll swim with you on my back, like a dolphin." She liked that.

The walls rose perpendicular on both sides. There were stalactites coming down from the roof, white and eerily threatening. I thought the grotto's silence and its greenish light creepy. Lucia was awed. Silent. "If you don't talk, you might see some glow-worms," Guido said. We went further in, the paddle silent in the still water.

"Look!" I whispered, pointing, and there were the glow-worms, tiny pinpoints of light above us.

"If you shout they go out," Guido said mischievously. "Shall I shout?"

"No. Don't spoil it." We slid silently along. The light was growing dim.

"There's the cave," whispered Guido, pointing.

I looked to our right and saw, behind a jumble of rocks, a narrow tunnel sloping away and upwards. "How far does it go?" I asked.

"I don't know," Guido replied carelessly. "We don't go far. Only far enough where we can see. This is where I leave the canoe."

"Oh! You've shut off the glow-worms!" exclaimed Lucia in dismay.

"You've seen them." Guido was matter of fact.

"Why are you leaving the canoe here?" I asked. I was a little concerned that a boy of nine should be allowed to play in such a potentially dangerous place. Donna had said the water was over Lucia's head. It was a pale greenish colour and the bottom was white but I could not easily judge its depth. It probably wasn't very deep.

"Thieves could get it if I left it outside." Guido's dark eyes were shining as he answered my question and I realised that thieves were a part of his game.

"You've talked and made the glow-worms go out," Lucia complained again.

"I have to answer people's questions," Guido retorted. He had taken hold of a spur of rock that jutted above and beyond the ledge. "You have to get out here."

The ledge ended in a slope down to the water. I clambered out and leant down to lift Lucia but she scrambled past me. Guido followed and between us we pulled the canoe out and dragged it up into the cave. Lucia had run ahead. I called to her and she came back swiftly. "I don't like it there. It's dark."

"You shouldn't have come, then," Guido told her, defending his playground. "You're too young."

"I'm not too young to see the glow-worms. I only don't want to see the cave."

I ventured farther in, but there was nothing to see. The walls were shiny with damp. Ahead there was darkness. I turned. Guido was already making his way along the ledge. I followed with Lucia clinging to my hand. "Careful, now," I said. I had joked about swimming out with the child on my back. Now I hoped very much it wouldn't happen. I walked sideways with my back to the wall so I could more easily hold on to Lucia's hand. As we came near to the entrance the sunlight took the eerie greenness away. I jumped down and lifted her in my arms. She looked down into my face, studying it.

"You're nice," she remarked.

I looked up into her round blue eyes and replied, "You're nice, too."

"Are you going to stay for the summer?"

We were walking towards Donna who was waiting on the grass. She answered for me. "The summer is nearly over, *carissima*, but Jane can stay as long as she likes because she is a sister."

"Oh." Lucia accepted the fact without question. Then, turning to Guido, announced with much pleasure: "Jane is a sister, Guido."

"Don't be silly," Guido retorted without acrimony. "Sisters wear long black dresses."

"A sister like Marisa," Donna explained.

There was a long silence while the children digested that. Donna watched their little faces, smilingly. "Did you enjoy your visit to the cave, Jane?"

"Lucia and I were a little awed," I confessed. "It's a boy's playground, I think. What about that cave?"

"Of course Andrew has explored it with a lantern. There are no passages leading out of it. It goes up into the cliff quite a way. It's dry up there. The children can't come to any harm."

Guido was staring at me. "What do you mean, Jane's a sister like Marisa?"

"Papa had her for a daughter before he met us."

Guido gave me a puzzled look. "Why didn't you come before?" he asked.

It was my turn to improvise. "Because I lived in London."

"Oh." And if Guido thought about it any more, he did not comment. I was established, just so easily, as a member of the family.

We climbed back up the hill. The late afternoon sun was shining directly on it now. We had to pause often for Lucia. After a while I lifted her in my arms and carried her. We arrived at the top, exhausted, where I put Lucia down and collapsed on a rock. Donna settled beside me, the children scampering off. "What a lovely life the children lead here," I said. I felt a touch of envy.

"It's nice to grow up by the sea, with boats," Donna agreed.

"Do you get storms?"

"Yes. Quite bad ones. But of course they know they can't come down here in a storm."

We looked out of the bay. "How calm it all is," she said. "How calm."

"Let's hope it stays that way." I wasn't talking about the ocean. She gave me a thoughtful look.

We found Andrew in a garden chair beneath a striped sun awning on the terrace. Maria was putting fruit drinks on the table. Andrew had an aperitif ready for Donna and me. I flopped down in one of the vacant chairs, wiping my perspiring forehead with the back of my hand. "What a life of ease and luxury you lead." The tranquil sea, the encompassing bushes, the brick walls that hid the terrace from prying eyes.

This was a hiding place, all right, I thought. Even a predatory caller like me, stepping over the gate, would be unlikely to find him.

"Ease and luxury!" He looked bemused. "I work very hard when the mood's on me—"

"—and at all hours," broke in Donna, smiling at him, affecting disapproval.

"Yes, that's true. But when my brain is tired, as it inevitably becomes, I stop work with a clear conscience. One would like to work office hours, but an artist's life is not like that."

"And what have you done today?" I thought I saw an expression of guilt touch his face briefly. He has not worked at all, I thought, concerned. He has been worrying. And then he said, "Nothing much, I'm afraid," and began to examine his nails. Donna went to stand behind him, resting her hands on his shoulders.

Lucia was demolishing a large glass of lemonade in thirsty gulps. She turned, wiped her red mouth with the back of her hand and announced with enormous pride, "Jane's a sister. Like Marisa."

I thought, but was not sure, that my father looked annoyed. Then Donna slid an arm through his and the expression went.

"They have to know," she said.

He looked at me. His face was grave. "I was not certain whether she was going to stay."

"I don't have to," I replied, immediately on edge.

"Now, now," cried Donna warmly but reprovingly, "you are making our new daughter feel unwanted, and I know you don't mean to. He means," she explained, turning to me as though translating a foreign language, "that you have unfortunately found us at an unhappy time. But that is not important. The important thing is that we have acquired a grown-up daughter just when we need one rather badly. Is that not so, Andrew?"

He gave Donna a dry look. "I hope we are being fair to her."

I realised what he was saying, or thought I did. If things went wrong for him, if the Bolivian millionaire produced his Raphael, proving conclusively that the one Andrew had put up for sale was a fake, I had found him not only to lose him again, but to get involved in the family's shame. Well, I had my own guilty feelings to contend with. I had brought an enemy into the camp of this dear family who had welcomed me so unsuspectingly.

Then I remembered he had not admitted ownership of the picture in Amsterdam. So, neither of them were being open with me. Perhaps they were, I thought again. Perhaps the clue lay in Donna's saying I found them at 'this unhappy time'. Perhaps that clue had been carefully placed for me to read.

I switched my thoughts away. An all-important requisite in a daughter, I thought, was loyalty. I said, "It's an ill wind that blows nobody any good. I wouldn't have been here if you hadn't been getting this publicity. I might never have found you."

"There you are," said Donna in her tranquil way. "That's the silver lining."

Donna and the children were to go to church at the Duomo. I did not ask if it was my father's Protestantism that kept him away, because it laid him open to having to say he was in hiding. I had thought it brave of him to have come to the hotel to meet me. That, I recognised, may mean he is more impulsive than he appears.

The children were very smart this morning, as was Donna, who wore a cinnamon coloured suit with a silk scarf richly patterned in greens, browns and golds tied loosely at her neck. Lucia and Marisa wore white socks and black patent leather shoes with buckles on the toes. Lucia looked like a doll with her fair curls clustering round her face. She was wearing a pinafore-type dress, not at all like the one she wore to school. This was handmade, of fine embroidered cotton, old fashioned to my eyes, but adding to the doll-like look. Marisa carried a missal. She looked very young for twelve in her short pleated skirt and white jumper, her dark hair brushed back and tied with a ribbon. Her skin, tanned from the summer sun, was pale coffee against the white. They were very different, these two daughters of my father, but only on the surface, for when one looked closely, the same face looked back.

They invited me to accompany them. "But you can't come like that," said Marisa, looking critically at my jeans.

"I'll change. I won't be long." We were on the terrace. It was another of those wonderful days, the sun hot in a bright blue sky. I started towards the door that on this level led into the salon.

"Don't feel obliged to come," Donna called after me.

I turned to say I would be happy to do so but Guido broke in, "Why should she not be obliged?" He, too, had that Sunday look. He wore a white shirt and a bow tie that gave him the look of a miniature grown-up. His hair was brushed back from his face today. I hoped it would flop forward again when he got out into the open air. He didn't look his usual self at all.

"Because she is not a Catholic," Donna said to him. "That's right, isn't it, Jane?" She smiled, ready to approve my Protestantism.

"It's a sin," said Marisa piously, "not to be a Catholic."

"Certainly it is not," retorted Donna, laughing.

I opened my mouth to say I was not a Catholic, then closed it again. Carl's mother was Italian. It was possible he was Catholic too, and therefore might be at the cathedral. I didn't want anyone to suggest I shouldn't go. I said, "I'll come with you. I'd very much like to." Then remembered Andrew and added swiftly, "If Andrew doesn't mind being left alone." I saw, too late, that he would have liked my company. It was in his face, a faint lifting of those fair, greying brows, an inner sigh. Perhaps he was at last thinking he might talk to me. But there was no turning back. The children were clustering round me excitedly.

"You can be a Catholic, I expect," said Guido consolingly.

"I think I'll just stay a heathen."

They were delighted. "Our papa is a heathen," contributed Lucia, knitting us together in a way that warmed my heart. Our papa. Had she included me, knowing since yesterday that I was a sister? I drove the nail home. "So, I'm his daughter. I'm a heathen too. But I will go with you this morning, and with pleasure."

"I will show you the Cloisters of Paradise," offered Guido magnanimously.

"If you would like to see them," Andrew corrected him.

"Oh yes. Do. I should be delighted."

"Byzantine-Arab," said Andrew, leaning back in his chair, looking up at me. "Do you know anything about architecture?"

"No, but I'm willing to learn," I replied, smiling down into Guido's eager face, thinking about the unlikelihood of an English boy of his age wanting to show me a church. Thinking, too, how little my father knew about me. I was sorely torn: wanting to go with the children; wanting to see Carl; wanting to stay with my father in case he was actually in a mood to talk. 'Do you know anything about architecture?' seemed such an odd question for a man to ask of his own daughter. But then, I wasn't a real daughter. Had not been one more than a few days. "Especially since I don't know about this historical stuff," I said.

"Do go with them," Andrew said. And then, indicating that he had seen my hesitation, "We'll have plenty of time to talk."

I hoped so. I dashed inside, took the stairs two at a time and changed quickly into the yellow blouse and skirt.

We hurried down the winding road into the town, Marisa holding one of my hands, Lucia the other, Guido walking with his mother behind, calling out to me interesting bits of information rather like a tourist guide. "The tomb of San Andrea is in the crypt, Jane, did you know?"

I didn't even know who San Andrea was, unless he was one of Christ's apostles, brother of Simon Peter, but I thought that one was variously said to be buried at Constantinople, and Scotland. I kept my ignorance to myself and marvelled at this little half-brother, feeling proud.

We joined the crowds hurrying through the piazza. There were some boys kicking a ball around. Nobody seemed to mind. The great cathedral was very beautiful this morning with the sun on its gilding. I looked up at the pointed arches; the various scenes from Christ's life depicted in mosaics. We jostled with the crowds on the steps.

I was intrigued at the way my family moved in and around with the locals, mingling with old women in black head-scarves and peasant dress, old men who looked like fisherfolk, as no doubt they were, their Sunday black grown shiny with the years. There were lots of little girls dressed like Lucia in white pinafores, and a handful of women quite as smart as Donna.

It was not the type of crowd I was accustomed to at home, those who walked in little twos and threes, greeting each other circumspectly with a polite good morning, then moving silently into our rather dull church. These children greeted friends with cries of genuine pleasure, as did Donna, but she did not introduce me. I recognised I was a complication. One does not say, 'She is Andrew's daughter,' in passing.

We hurried with the crowds who were hurrying also, though

I did not know why. There was no shortage of seating. The interior of the cathedral was magnificent. I gazed around at the holy pictures with awe. Christ with angels. Fat cherubs, pink and white and gilt. I thought perhaps I was missing quite a lot by being, as I had said, a heathen.

We filed into our seats. In a way, as perhaps one does by osmosis in a strange church, I understood what was going on, though the Mass was mainly incomprehensible. I absorbed the richness, felt the sense of drama, watched and smelt the swinging incense, listened to the droning liturgy, admired the candles. I copied the genuflexions, knelt down, stood, with the congregation. I absorbed the great solemnity of the occasion. When the family – that was how I was thinking of them, the family – went up with the crowd to the altar rail for communion I sat and watched them, feeling content, though still, and especially here, a stranger.

It was when we were out on the steps again that I saw Carl. He stood a head taller than the Italians. He came up to us, smiling, and held out his hand formally, as though he had never kissed me, I thought wryly. Then he shook hands with Donna and each of the children in turn, and we all came down the wide steps together. Because the children were chattering I did not hear what he was saying to my stepmother, but she turned as we reached the street and said, "You didn't say you were going out to dinner with Carl tonight."

"I'm not," I said, avoiding Carl's eyes. "I thought you might not want me to go out when I had just arrived. He did ask me but I turned him down."

She smiled her warm smile. "Oh, how unkind. It happens to be convenient," she went on, "for your father and I are to dine with friends. We would have taken you, I'm sure they wouldn't mind, but Carl's invitation might be more to your taste. Our friends don't speak any English at all. It could be very boring for you."

"Yes, of course." I wondered why she was literally throwing me at Carl's head when she knew he was to marry Evelina. Could it be that she carried the edict of minding her own business to extraordinary limits? I'll find a way out of it, I thought. What on earth would my reception be? I had thought him sensitive. I was wrong. He must be totally lacking in sensitivity.

"I'll pick you up at seven-thirty," he said.

I glared at him.

"That will suit you, Jane, won't it?" Donna asked. "We shall be going out at seven. Come, darlings." She gathered up the children and started off along the street. I followed, feeling disturbed.

Chapter Seven

After Sunday lunch Andrew and Donna went off for their siesta and I wandered down to the beach with the children, made sand-castles with Lucia and talked to Marisa, getting to know her. Guido had gone off to the grotto to get the canoe and meet his friends. Marisa told me about her school, the nuns at the *convento*, her friends. They had lots of relations, it seemed, but they lived in Rome. She did not mention the fact that her relations were all Italian. I suppose it had not occurred to her that there was anything amiss about not having English relatives.

We swam, then I sunbathed while the children built more sand-castles. Donna came to join us later in the afternoon. We sat together on the stone seat watching Lucia play. Marisa swam then lay on the sand in the sun reading a book. The bay was empty, until the steamer from Sorrento came swiftly and quietly in, leaving a trail of feathery grey smoke across the sky, making for the pier which was out of sight from our little cove. As it disappeared a speedboat suddenly leaped out from behind the fold in the cliff and with throttle open roared across the water, heading in our direction. About a hundred yards out the engines cut out and the boat came sliding in towards the beach. A man stood up in the stern.

"Ach!" said Donna, or something like that. She rose, smoothing her skirt.

"A reporter?" I suggested. He was dressed in slacks and a blazer. He looked too formal to be a holidaymaker.

"I expect so," she said resignedly as she went to meet him. I could see they were arguing. He gestured towards the villa. Marisa jumped up and went to stand beside her mother. "*Privato.*" I heard her say, more forcefully. "*Privato.*" After a while, reluctantly, the man turned and climbed back into the boat. The engine burst into life and they raced back across the water. I could see why Maria had given me such short shrift that day I climbed over the gate. One could get very tired of this sort of thing. When Donna returned her face was strained.

This is ridiculous, I said to myself. Why should she go through it week after week? I decided then and there to tackle her. I said, "If this picture in Amsterdam has nothing to do with my father, why doesn't he come out and say so?"

She looked across at the child playing in the sand. "It is his way," she said.

"What do you mean, Donna?"

"Just that it is Andrew's way."

"What is his way? To never explain?" I wondered if it was this attitude that had driven him to leave England all those years ago. "To hide his head in the sand?" I asked.

"No," she replied and smiled at me. She had a very sweet smile. "You don't know him very well yet."

"Donna," I said, keeping my exasperation under control, "either he sent that picture to Amsterdam, or he didn't. It's easy enough to say yes or no. If he is completely blameless—"

Donna's face closed. She said in a quiet and carefully controlled voice, "If your father put this picture up for sale, and I am not saying he did, then it was in the honest belief it was genuine. That is all that matters. *All* that matters, Jane," she repeated. "He was innocent of the other thing that happened in England, and if he is concerned with the Raphael, then he will be shown to be innocent of that, too."

I was deeply touched by my stepmother's devotion. "Just loving a man doesn't make him good," I said, my voice gentle.

"If you love a man enough and have sufficient faith in him," Donna replied, "you can keep his head above water in times of stress and strain. Isn't it all that matters, so far as his family is concerned?"

I could only think she was the perfect wife for a complex man. I hoped that was what he was. Complex. Only that.

"Shall we go up?" she suggested. "We shall be having tea shortly and you will want to shower and change for dinner. Maria makes English cakes and scones. You may find them a little different. Italian ingredients are not entirely similar to English. But she's a good cook."

"I know," I said warmly. "She made the most wonderful croissants for breakfast. Croissants, in Italy!"

"I noticed you don't like the rolls. It's true they can be hard. We are accustomed to them."

"She made croissants specially for me? I didn't realise that. How kind."

We went up the winding path and steps in silence. I was thinking of what Donna had said about my father. I had to respect her reasoning, but my heart was heavy. He must have sent that picture to Amsterdam. I could not imagine, if he was innocent, why he wouldn't say so.

I went to my room. There was a telephone on the table, and on a shelf below, a directory. I looked up the Bs, and there it was. Beaumont. It's all very well to let clever Carl Beaumont down, I said to myself, but I cannot be discourteous to his mother. I felt it was safe to ring. There was little chance of his picking up the telephone, for he could hardly be in Salerno now and pick me up in Amalfi at seven.

I dialled. The signora answered. I covered my intentions by asking first to speak to Carl. "He is not here," she said, and recognising the English voice, "Is that Jane?"

I said it was. "The message is actually for you," I said. "I'm sorry, but I'm unable to accept your kind invitation for this evening. I hope it won't inconvenience you."

The signora's natural courtesy scarcely covered the fact that she was vastly relieved. "I will give him the message," she said.

I said goodbye, had a swift shower, washed the sand out of my hair and changed into the blue dress that was good enough for dining alone. There were dozens of restaurants in Amalfi. I would sneak out before he arrived and find one off the beaten track. I felt depressed, but I could not go to his mother's. I would have dearly loved a candlelit dinner with him. I wandered down to the end of the passage and went through the door that led into the garden. Above the rockery on my right lay the path that ran between the lemon and orange trees that were close to Andrew's studio.

I thought I heard a muffled sound from that direction, like a cough or sneeze. I glanced at my watch. Perhaps he had forgotten the time. I headed up the path. The door to the studio was open. I was about to call when I heard a woman's voice. I paused, not deliberately listening, but wondering whether I should intrude. Then I heard the voice say, "It is absolutely without value. It is worth even less than you gave me for it."

Who was that? I recognised the voice. Surely not Evelina?

"I implore you to withdraw it before the thing goes any further," she was saying. "My father is already upset about the rumours. When he finds out it really did come from you—"

Then Andrew's voice, "You sold me the picture, my dear, and your involvement ends there. Your name will never be mentioned."

"It is your name I am worried about."

He laughed, but the laugh was warm and generous. "Why should you worry? What am I to you but one of your father's writers?"

I stood there rooted to the ground. Stunned. Evelina! They were still talking. Evelina's voice was raised but she spoke in Italian now. I turned and crept back. This is weird, I said to myself. Because I didn't feel like facing the family I went back to my room and, kneeling on the elegant sofa, leaned my elbows on the windowsill, staring down into the baked garden with its neat terraces, its miniature stone walls, the bright geraniums and bougainvillaea, the dark green shrubs and the giant cactus with its brilliant vermillion fruit. The sun was sinking towards the blue horizon and down in the garden I could hear Maria singing.

I felt angry with Evelina, and also with Andrew. I wondered if, while we were sitting over tea, she would say something that would give me an opening. I wondered what, given the opening, I would say.

A child's voice called, "Jane! Tea time."

I took a deep breath and made my way up the stairs. Maria was laying out the children's mugs and teacups on a table in the salon, as Donna called it. Three cups, not four. "Almond cake today," said Donna, pointing to a very attractive-looking golden cake in the middle of the table. "This is more lethal than your English almond cake. We have a delicious local almond liqueur called Amoretta which Maria puts in."

"What's lethal?" asked Marisa.

"Poison," said Guido.

An uproar ensued, and much laughter. Donna poured the tea. "Now, where is your father?" She addressed Guido.

He wasn't listening. His eyes were greedily surveying the cake. "Can I have a bit now"

"Wouldn't you like to find your father? His tea will get cold."

It was clear to me that Donna didn't know she had a guest for tea. I was about to say I would go and look for him when heard his footsteps and then he was standing at the door looking in.

"Ah! Tea," he said, rubbing his hands. "Just what I need."

I looked past him, waiting for Evelina to appear, for him to say he had a guest and could someone bring another cup. He simply went to the table, picked up his tea and retired to a comfortable chair.

"And how did you enjoy your swim?" he asked, looking at me.

I scarcely heard him, or rather my scattered wits precluded my understanding what he was saying.

"What is the matter, Jane?" Donna asked.

"Nothing," I said and smiled. At least my mouth smiled. I was wishing I had not made that telephone call to Signora Beaumont. I needed to see Carl. Immediately.

"It's the poisoned cake," shouted Guido. "She doesn't want to eat it. She thinks she'll die. There's more for us." He drummed his bare feet on the carpet. Everyone laughed and I said I was sorry to deprive him, but I couldn't wait to try the cake.

As soon as tea was over I slipped down to my room and picked up the telephone again. I had made a note of the Beaumont number on the little pad considerately placed by the phone. I dialled it again.

"Yes," said Carl's mother, she had given him my message. "He telephoned a little while ago."

"So he isn't there?"

"What is it now, Jane?" She sounded impatient, as well she might.

"Nothing," I said, "it doesn't matter." I might have managed that better, I thought as I hung up. I telephoned the Hotel Maria Convento. Signor Beaumont was out, the desk clerk said.

There was nothing to do now but keep to my original resolution and go out myself. I could not confess this silliness to Andrew and Donna. Besides, Maria had been told I would be out and therefore would not be prepared to feed me. I waited for Donna and Andrew to go.

Ten minutes later I left the villa and set out on the winding road that led down the hill. No wonder my father chose to live here, I thought, in this little white town with its ever-present feeling of the richness of the past, its proximity to the ancient and art-embellished cities of Rome and Florence, its history. What better atmosphere in which to paint and put together those lovely Ben Tyrill books? St Andrew the apostle it was, the patron saint of fisherfolk, whom Guido had told me was buried in the cathedral. I had checked that out with Donna. She said also that the crypt held the bones of historians and musicians. If Andrew had lost his English heritage, he had surely gained magnificently in return. These were my thoughts as I set out to look for my lonely dinner.

I came almost to the town then turned back towards the tunnel. There was a tall stone wall on my left and some steep stone steps in the cliff. I had noticed them before, and also the hoarding indicating that a hotel lay out of sight in what must be a scoop in the hill. I hesitated, then decided to investigate. I crossed the road and entered an antiquated lift, a rickety old thing. It dawdled upwards, groaning painfully, frightening me a little with its clangs and its rattling.

The lift gates opened on to a pathway that ran into a beautiful garden. The hotel, all brown stone and archways, had a long terrace that trailed off into a covered way bright with purple bougainvillaea. There were people at little tables on the terrace, and in the garden, relaxing beneath lemon trees that were trained prettily over umbrella-shaped wire, their yellow fruit gleaming against the dark leaves.

I wandered along the stone flagging that was warm still from the heat of the day, and sat down at a small table beside an enormous Ali Baba jar sprouting geraniums out of the top.

The people at the next table to mine glanced up in brief curiosity before returning their attention to their drinks and each other. A waiter in a white coat came towards me carrying a silver tray. I ordered a Campari.

I must have stayed a long time in that scented garden, lingering over the same drink while the ice in it melted away and the sun went down into a silent sea. Bright orange pomegranates in the tree above my table faded into the blackness of their leaves. The great cross in the people's cemetery on the hill burst into diamond brightness, and the sea dimmed in the dusk. It was night.

Lost in admiration, lost in my thoughts, I was startled by a movement, and glanced up to see the waiter at my table with that look waiters wear when one has sat too long over a single drink.

It was then I saw Carl. He sat at one of the little white-clothed tables on the narrow terrace, close beneath the arches that ran along the front of the hotel. Because there was a small light in the vine directly overhead, and a pair of candles on the table, I could see his face clearly, but his head was close to that of a woman whose face I could not see. They must have been there for some time because there was an uncorked bottle on the table, and food.

My first sensation was one of anger that he could accept my refusal without protest, and immediately ask another woman out. Perhaps sensing, as one does, that someone was watching them, he looked up and straight at me. At first he did not recognise me – the tiny light above my own table was dim – but gradually I saw suspicion dawn on his face, then certainty. He said a word to the girl, she turned, then he rose and came with long strides across the paving stones towards me.

"Jane!" He spoke with consternation and warmth, and my silly heart did a flip. "What are you doing here all alone?" He pulled a chair up and sat directly opposite me with his back to the girl, leaning across the table, looking at me with anxious eyes.

I tried to smile. What are *you* doing here? was what I wanted to ask. And with *her*!

He looked up and saw the waiter hovering. Immediately, he became businesslike. He took the chit and paid.

I said, "That's very kind of you. But please—"

He raised a hand to silence me, and got to his feet. "You must eat with us."

"You've got company," I said, and flushed as I heard the bitterness in my voice.

"It's only Evelina."

"Evelina?"

My utter astonishment startled him. "Why not? You turned me down." That mobile mouth turned up, then down.

I stared at him in mind-blocked silence until, with a light chuckle, he said, "I got your message. I couldn't see any point in ringing for an explanation, so I jumped into the car and set out to collect you as arranged. But I ran into Evelina, in the town. At least, I saw her car and paused to say hello. She wasn't doing anything, so we went for a drink and I decided that—" his eyes suddenly twinkled and his lips twitched "—since you didn't want to have dinner with me and she did . . . Come and join us, anyway. You can't sit here all by yourself."

He pulled me to my feet. Evelina was watching us with intense interest. She sat very erect, very slim in a cream dress of some thick silky material, her fingers touching the stem of her wine glass. She watched me all the way up to the table.

"Good evening," I said.

"We did not expect to see you here," she replied. With the briefest gesture she indicated to a hovering waiter that he might bring another chair. I sat down, feeling distinctly uncomfortable. Carl took an enormous menu from the waiter, then half-closing it, said directly to me, "We have ordered *hors d'œuvres* and mussels in white wine. Do you like the sound of that, Jane?"

I would have liked anything when he spoke to me like that, gently and persuasively.

Looking back, I do not remember very much about that dinner because all the while I was trying to find an opening to broach the subject of Evelina's visit to the Villa Passerina. It came right at the end.

"It has been a lovely day," Evelina said, and quick as a flash I replied, "I am sorry I missed you at my father's villa. I overheard you talking to him, but didn't go in because I felt certain you would be there for tea. Why did you disappear so suddenly?"

Evelina looked astonished. She opened her big eyes wide, and her mouth. She had pretty teeth, so even they looked almost unreal. "Me?" she repeated, her voice high and strange. "Not me, Jane. I haven't seen your father for ages."

"But it was your voice, and I heard—"

She cut in with a quick laugh, and at the same moment rose from the table. "Not *my* voice," she said very firmly. Then, adopting a casual tone, "Come, Jane, there is a room inside where we can powder our noses. It is late. I did not intend to stay out so long."

Evelina walked ahead, leading me down the wide passage. Then she turned a corner and pushed open a door marked *Signoras*. She turned and held the door open for me. There was no one there. She sat down on a narrow stool before the looking glass, indicating that I take the only chair.

"Listen," she said, her voice clipped now, and very business-like, "Andrew is in trouble, and there is something you can do for him."

"Yes?"

"Make him withdraw that Raphael picture. It is not genuine. It is only a matter of time before the Bolivian millionaire produces the real one, and Andrew will be accused of trying to sell another forgery."

I said, noting how tight her face had become, noting the nervous drumming of her fingers on her knee, "Evelina, you sold this picture to Andrew."

She laughed. "But how ridiculous!"

"You did." I was quite sure of myself on that point. '*You sold me the picture, my dear—*' I had overheard Andrew say it. I knew I was not mistaken. I would have staked my life on the fact that it was her. I watched her face in the mirror, half eclipsed by her shining hair that had fallen forward as though she were hiding behind it. Then she shook it back and lifted her head. Her fingers stopped drumming. She looked stricken for a moment. I thought she had decided to confess. Then she seemed to take herself in hand. A veil came down. "It really has nothing to do with me," she said lightly, the vulnerability gone.

"Then why are you so anxious for him to withdraw it?" I asked. I was aware of hounding her. But how does one get to the truth, otherwise? I had brought Carl into my father's life. There was no turning the clock back, but I owed him more than an apology. I owed him the privacy that Carl could take away.

Evelina glanced at herself in the mirror, discarded the fear she saw and put a smile on her pretty face. "You must know," she said lightly, "my father is his publisher, and if there is one thing he hates, it's scandal."

"But surely that is a matter between your father and Andrew. What has it to do with you, if you didn't sell him the picture?" I was watching her very closely. The nervousness was still there, more fear than nervousness, I thought, but under control. She was very good at covering up, but I had seen the chink in her armour.

"My father would not like to speak to him about such a matter."

"Oh, I don't know," I retorted, still watching her like a hawk. "I should think, since they are friends as well as business colleagues, that he would find it very easy to have a word."

I was being too harsh. I saw a flash of panic in those dark Italian eyes. Then she took herself in hand again. I saw her in the mirror straighten her back, lift her head so that the silky hair that had fallen forward again slipped back. "My father did not know, when he began to publish Andrew's books, about what had happened in London before he came to Italy," she said.

"Oh, come on!" I retorted in exasperation. "Are you really saying that if he had known he would have refused the Ben Tyrill books?"

She shrugged and turned away. "How do I know? What has this to do with me?"

"Precisely," I retorted. "That's what I said. Andrew's affairs can't have anything to do with you unless you sold him that Raphael *Madonna and Child*."

She sat in silence, looking somehow defeated. I thought I had gone too far. But I couldn't stop now. I said, "Why did you not want Carl to know you had been to the Villa Passerina?"

She stood up, glanced at herself in the mirror and took a lipstick and a little brush from her bag. She brushed her lips lightly, giving herself thinking time. I felt I was on the edge of something. That she either almost trusted me or was desperate enough to confide in me. Then the decision went against. She replied distantly, "It ought to be very obvious to you. Carl wants to interview him. He would think it uncooperative of me not to give him an introduction."

She had said some pretty silly things tonight, but that took the cake. "I am the one who introduced them, as you very well know. Come on," I said and stalked out of the door. "Carl will be wondering what has happened to us."

He was waiting at the end of the path where the steps began and the old, clanking lift lay. "You were a mighty long time," he remarked, looking curiously from one of us to the other. I managed a smile. "Just chatting."

Evelina, keeping her face averted from me, gathered her strength and slid the heavy door open.

"Hey!" Carl protested, "Leave that to me." But he was too late. She stepped inside the lift and we followed. Its noisy clanks and scraping as we descended precluded talk. We stepped out. "That's my car," Carl said indicating an exceedingly smart red convertible with a black hood that was parked nearby.

"Is this the one you leave at your mother's villa?"

"Yes. It's got character, don't you think?" He unlocked the door. "It's a Karmann Ghia 1967," he said with pride.

I had no idea what a Karmann Ghia was. I agreed it had great character. It was the kind of car I would have expected him to own.

"I'll walk," I said. "There's no point in running me such a short way up the hill and having to turn round in the narrow road." There wasn't much room for an extra passenger, anyway. "You take Evelina. Thanks for the meal."

Evelina said, "Take her. I'll walk. Thank you, Carl." She reached up and kissed him swiftly on the cheek, then made off.

"Hey, what's going on?" Now I had the opportunity to tell him the truth I didn't have anything to tell, for exposing Evelina's visit, as I had intended, would only be a confirmation that the Raphael – fake Raphael? – had indeed been sent to Amsterdam by Andrew. I had to have time to think.

He said, "Her car isn't far away." He raised his voice. "Hey, Evelina!" She paused and he dashed across the road after her. They came back, she reluctantly, Carl imprisoning her with an arm through her elbow. I climbed into the tiny seat at the back. She looked a little resentful, as without a glance at me she slipped into the front passenger seat. He started the engine, swung the car round and swept off into the blackness of the tunnel. We shot through the darkened town and roared up the hill on the other side, then stopped in the road below the Hotel Maria Convento.

"There we are," he said and I saw a small red Fiat parked beneath a lamppost. So he had happened to run into her! He had done no such thing, I said to myself indignantly. She had been visiting him at his hotel. She didn't get out immediately. She turned to Carl and spoke in a flood of Italian, deliberately excluding me. I wasn't put out. I probably deserved it. I gave my attention to her little car. It was by no means new. I was surprised.

She climbed out. "I dare say you will want to move into the front," she said distantly, holding the door open, not looking at me.

"Thank you." I stepped out on to the road. "Goodnight, Evelina." I was feeling sorry for her, wishing I knew the nature of the raw nerve I had touched.

She said goodnight without turning her head then deliberately, it seemed to me, went round to the other side, bent down and kissed Carl again. We waited until she had started her car and moved off down the road.

To my astonishment, he ran back into the road and set off in the opposite direction to the villa.

"Hey!" I exclaimed in alarm. "Where are you going?"

"To my mother's place."

"But Carl, we were asked there for dinner!"

"So, the least we can do is turn up for a drink." His tone was bland. "I told Mama I would be bringing you, in spite of your telephone call, and I was, as I said, on the way to collect you when I ran into Evelina."

I let that pass. I was learning that when people had secrets it did no good to badger them. Maybe Evelina had gone to the hotel after her visit to the Villa Passerina in the hope of persuading him to leave Andrew alone. I didn't think that bawling him out would upset him in the least but I knew it would avail me nothing, and possibly make me cross. "Then what made you change your mind?" I asked sweetly. "Evelina's charm?"

He laughed. We roared up the hill on the road to Salerno. "Since we're into questions," he said, keeping his eyes on the road, "how does it happen that you can't come out to dinner at my mother's place and yet you can get dressed up and sit in a hotel garden drinking all by yourself?"

"Drinking?" I repeated sharply. I suppose I was emotionally *distrait* by this time. "I was having an apéritif. And I was hiding, if you must know, because I didn't want to explain to Donna why I wasn't going out with you."

"And why were you not going out with me?"

"Because you're engaged to Evelina Lambardini." How bitter I sounded. He changed gear, raged up another of those steep rises. That was the moment, before he replied, to say, *Evelina sold that painting to my father*. I didn't.

He swung the car round a bend. "I get the picture," he said.

I settled back in the seat. It seemed sensible to change the subject. "I can't imagine that your mother will want to see us, three hours late?"

"She's very flexible."

I wondered if Italian hostesses didn't mind being left with dinner. I could imagine what would happen if I did this to one of my English friends. But things were different here. The signora would not have cooked the dinner. And I had no doubt she could well afford to throw it out. I guessed money could make one more forgiving.

Chapter Eight

"And how are you getting on with this father who treated you so badly?"

"Well," I replied, remembering he had said he was here to cover my meeting with Andrew. I couldn't entirely rule out the fact that that was the truth. I supposed it was possible he was covering the meeting as well as digging out the dirt about the painting.

"He has convinced you it was all for the best?"

Was that a touch of cynicism in his tone? "A woman's view is different from that of a man," I said. "He seems to have considered he had good reason for what he did. I have to remember my birth occurred at the same time as he left the country. If you're being critical of him, you might remember it was a very unhappy time for him. His partner had died. It would seem the art establishment was gunning for him." I felt better for that show of loyalty, remembering the trouncing I had given Andrew the day we met.

"Oh sure," Carl replied in the kind of voice one uses when totally disagreeing but not wanting to say so outright. I felt the Italian half of him was in the ascendant and like Donna he found it inexplicable that a man would choose to never see his child until she was old enough to look him up herself. I was English and I thought it inexplicable, too. But there were times when I accepted the fact that he was a very complicated man, perhaps deeply scarred by events that he had not been able to combat. Considerations of my stepfather's greed circled round in my mind. My mother's disloyalty, or weakness, or confusion. Can one really love two men equally? I suppose I had to believe it.

"It was all rather a mess," I said, explaining my tumbling thoughts to myself.

Carl, he who had so recently kissed Evelina, took a hand from the steering wheel to lay it over mine. And then we were swinging in at that gateway and there was the imposing Villa Adriana, its pink stone pillars warm and pretty in the floodlights that the car had activated.

"I left a file of important papers here," he said as he switched the engine off. "I had intended taking them back to the hotel after dinner. The dinner we didn't have here. So I had to make this trip."

I breathed a sigh of relief. I couldn't imagine that we were going to get any sort of reception, turning up like this. "You might have said that before."

"I wanted to punish you."

I laughed. That was fair enough. "So, is your mother expecting us now?"

"Of course. I telephoned her while you were having that long *tête-à-tête* with Evelina." He looked at me thoughtfully. "You haven't told me what that was about."

"Girls' talk." I was saved by Signora Beaumont coming out of the front door and beginning to descend the steps.

Carl jumped out. "*Ciao, Mama*. Better late than never."

She smiled and if that smile was a little stiff, it nevertheless held warmth for her son. She kissed him. "Good evening, Jane," she said, turning to me.

We shook hands. I noticed her mouth was a little thin. I did not blame her for being angry, but at the same time I couldn't help comparing her to my warmhearted stepmother. Signora Beaumont was like a sharp-eyed, beautiful bird. "I am sorry you couldn't come to dine," she said. Her voice was courteous. There was not the faintest reproof in her tone or manner. She set me at my ease.

"I hope we didn't put you out," I said.

"Not at all. Are you enjoying your stay in Amalfi?" She turned to lead us inside.

I thought it an odd question, since she knew my circumstances. And then I wondered if that was her way of saying she did not intend to pry. For that I could be grateful. "Very much, thank you."

We went into a rather grand hall. There was a glittering chandelier, a marble staircase, some very expensive looking antique tables, a sofa that looked as though no one had ever dared sit on it. I couldn't help wondering how Carl's father lived in London. We went into a drawing room – I was learning to call them *salons* – with lots of comfortable chairs and an enormous sofa. I felt this one had been used, if carefully.

There were some rather beautiful pictures on the walls and more of those very good antiques. Foreign, I guessed. Well, naturally, not English. Not necessarily Italian either. A wonderful marquetry cabinet made of pretty walnut decorated with flower paintings. I guessed that was Dutch. The mirror frames were heavily carved and gilded. There were photographs with gilt metal mounts. The bigger pieces of furniture had impressive ball-and-claw feet. It was a lovely room. Rather ornate, but lovely all the same.

A maid brought us coffee and liqueurs. I tasted the Amoretta that Maria so extravagantly put into her cake, and licked my lips appreciatively. Carl laughed and filled my glass again. "You're not driving," he said. "You don't have to worry."

The signora talked to me as a tourist, not as a potential friend. Did I know the ancient Romans had their summer houses at Amalfi? That the original roads were built by them? Had I seen the Cloisters of Paradise adjoining the dome of the cathedral? They were well worth a visit. That kind of thing. She was kind, but she had no intention of letting me in.

It was nearly half past one when we rose to go. "Is that the time?" I exclaimed in consternation. "Heavens, I hope we haven't outstayed our welcome."

"Not at all," Carl's mother replied graciously. "I go to bed late." She turned enquiringly to her son. "You have to collect some papers?"

"Ah, yes."

He went out and we remained in silence for a moment, listening to his footsteps receding along the marble hall, then Signora Beaumont stepped forward and looking hard into my face said in a quiet voice that might not be overheard even if Carl came suddenly back into the room, "I asked you here tonight because I have something to say to you. I am sure my son has not told you, but I think you should know he is to marry Evelina Lambardini."

I was silent for a moment, completely taken aback. I could have said I knew but I sensed that meant laying myself open to the question as to why I was here with him, ringing him up twice in an afternoon, etcetera. It seemed prudent to stay mute.

"I can see he is attracted to you because you are English," his mother went on, "and of course he is half English, and English educated, but it is important that he should marry an Italian girl."

"To please you?" I cannot imagine why I should have snapped back like that. Yes, I do know. Knew then. Hadn't I been contemplating, on the drive over, the bleak areas of my life? Howard in those early years pretending to want me. Andrew pretending he hadn't. Okay, I was an adult and I ought to have been able to deal with rejection, but I hadn't – quite. Plenty of people go for counselling on lesser issues. I found myself facing the fact that I loved Carl for his warmth, his attention, his particular pretence, of loving me.

"It would please me very much," she said, rightly ignoring my petty quip. "Young men can be a little careless with a girl's emotions. I thought it only right to warn you."

"I'm scarcely acquainted with him," I said. "As you know, he picked me up on the train." A lash to make her flinch. That was what I would call the human element.

"That's why I have said this," she returned smoothly. "You know nothing about him. How could you, as you said, having met on the train." She chose a nicer way of putting it. "My family and the Lambardinis have been great friends for a very long time. I've known Evelina since she was a little girl. It has always been understood—"

"Please," I protested, my face scarlet with embarrassment at my behaviour as well as hers. "Why should you speak to me like this? Maybe Italian girls take this kind of thing from their parents, but I am not Italian. I am twenty-six. And Carl is older, I'm sure. We're adults."

She was unmoved by my reaction. She spoke gently. "Because there is a saying – 'a flower starts with a bud'."

She was no fool, this beautiful signora. She knew I was in love with her son. I think that was what made her speak. The fact that we had known each other only a few days was irrelevant, and perhaps she could see that. I thought she was afraid of me.

And then he came back. There was a brown paper package under his arm. He said, “Okay, let’s go,” and bent over to kiss his mother goodbye.

She held out a hand to me. “Goodbye.” She avoided using my name.

“Goodnight, Signora Beaumont,” I said. “And thank you.”

She came out with us and stood beside one of the impressive pillars, watching as we sped away. It was dark on the road. The streetlights had been extinguished and we seemed to have the night to ourselves. “What have you got in that parcel?” I asked.

“I told you I had to come for papers.”

“But they are not papers in the parcel.” I began to laugh. “It is a round bundle. It looks like clothes.”

He grinned. “How very observant of you.”

“Then, if you did not need to collect papers, why did we call on your mother?”

“You are being very blunt tonight, Jane.”

If only he knew! Or had he been listening outside the door? What had he made of our exchange? His mother’s part in it? I thought if he had overheard then he was infinitely loyal and kind. I loved him for it. Loved him. You don’t have to know people for years to love them. You can fall in love on a train; when a man is holding you to ransom; threatening to expose your father; throwing you to a lion in the person of a hostile mother; behaving the way a man ought not to behave if he loves you. And then I thought, well, I don’t know. If he’s a man of steel who knows his own mind . . . Knows where he’s going . . .

I turned to look at him. He turned, too. We smiled at each other. When he ran the car to a stop outside the Villa Passerina he switched off the engine and took me in his arms. Of course I should have rejected him. *You’re somebody else’s fiancé*, I should have said. *You’re here to ruin my father*. I didn’t. I lifted my face and kissed him, slowly, sweetly and willingly. I was a child, stealing cake from the kitchen. An alcoholic, snatching at the gin before my minder could remove it.

I wanted to say, *I love you*. I tried very hard to stop myself and in the end, won that battle. After all, he hadn’t said he loved me. How could he? That would have been taking his cheating on Evelina far too far. He was a cheat. He was using me to get at my father. He was going to have me thrown out of the Villa Passerina. Out, for all time, of my newfound family. At that moment I did not care. Just being in his arms was enough for me. I thought I would die of happiness.

I slept well, dreaming wondrous dreams. I was swimming in the bay with Carl, crying out with happiness at being with him. *I feel as though I've been with you forever*, I said. *I hope this will never end*. He didn't answer, but he smiled.

I wakened early, as usual, and climbed out of bed. I loved these mild Mediterranean mornings, the sun coming up behind the range of mountains, striking the horizon first, then the island of Capri, dispersing its mists and drawing a light skein, like silk, across the dark morning water. I crossed the cool tiled floor in my nightdress. The bay was spattered with white foam. Behind the thick walls of the villa I had not heard the wind.

A squall blacked out the horizon. There were no fishing boats. That wind was leaping and dancing across the garden, snatching frail blossoms, laying them on the ground. The one orange tree within my range of vision stood almost denuded. As I watched in dismay golden fruit leaped out of its green shelter and rolled down the slope. The low-growing foliage bowing and dipping at the edge of the small lawn was bright with oranges.

I dressed quickly and hurried up to the kitchen where I found a basket hanging behind the door. I came back, put on my light jacket, climbed over the windowsill and set about gathering up the fruit. The wind tore at my hair, buffeted me. I loved it. It set my senses singing. I slipped back over the sill and went upstairs with my pickings. The villa was silent. 'If the sun is shining,' Carl had said when he dropped me the night before, 'I'll be swimming. Meet me there.' The sun was certainly not shining but I was on a high from the foolishness of the night before. I had to be out and about.

I swung off down the hill heading for the beach. The wind whipped along the streets, spiralling dust and rubbish and leaves. The water on the front rose in angry leaps, tearing up the sloping sands and pounding against the wall. It was almost inconceivable that only the day before I had stood here beneath a cloudless sky. Prudent fishermen had been down in the night to haul their boats in. I pulled my collar close, walked to the end of the sea wall and back, looked up at the hill where the Hotel Maria Convento lay, looking for a tall figure striding down the road. I walked up and down, breathing the boisterous salty wind deep down into my lungs, telling myself I was not disappointed, that I was enjoying my solitary little morning adventure. But when I was ready to go back I lingered on.

He did not come. It was a slower, less jaunty walk back to the villa.

"*Ah, Signorina*!" Maria met me at the door, scolding me noisily in Italian for going out in such weather. *"Fa cattivo tempo*." Look! I was damp with spray! My feet! Look at the sand! My hair was wet. We had become friends through an intimate study of sign language. She had a limited command of English. I had heard the best of it that day I climbed over the gate. She had considerable experience of getting rid of people. The family talked Italian to her.

I allowed her to take my jacket and lead me into the kitchen where she poured me some delicious milky coffee and then produced piping hot croissants from the oven.

"*Grazie di tutta la sua gentilezza,* Maria." The children were teaching me small talk. She beamed. She liked me to have a go.

It was a big kitchen, old-fashioned as kitchens in grand houses tend to be when the lady of the house does not cook. There was a long, heavy wooden table in the centre of the room, a huge range, some hard chairs, and copper pots and pans hanging from the ceiling. The floor was made of serviceable-looking brown tiles.

I pulled up one of the chairs and helped myself to a croissant. "Butter?" I made stroking movements with my knife.

She threw up her hands in horror. *Il burro*! On these rich croissants!

I stuck to my guns and she produced an enormous slab of butter, shaking her head violently.

"Maria, you are a wonderful cook!" I said sucking up to her, hoping to mollify her for showing such greed, or bad manners, or both.

Donna came in. Maria left off cutting her vegetables and, waving a dangerous-looking knife in the air, addressed her volubly. “Six!” exclaimed my stepmother. “You have eaten six of Maria’s croissants! And with butter! She is horrified.” But Donna was laughing.

“I was hungry. And what’s wrong with putting butter on them?”

“Nothing,” said Donna, the perfect hostess. “Put on them anything you like.” She bent down and kissed me on either cheek.

Drawn by the laughter, the children rushed in, dressed and ready for school, satchels in hand. They wore coats this morning and the girls were sporting cute little berets. Winter, it seemed, was here. I thought they looked sweet. They heard the story and expressed awe. “I’ve been a greedy pig,” I said. They liked that. “Greedy pig,” they repeated pleasurably, casting sly looks at their mother.

“Come on,” said Donna, “it’s time for you to go.”

They went off repeating, “Greedy pig,” rolling the words over their little tongues. I had a vision of them getting into serious trouble at the *convento*.

Andrew came in also dressed for winter in a wool jumper and cords. “Rosy cheeks,” he said. “I see you’re a morning constitutional girl.”

Donna told him, laughing, that I had eaten six croissants with butter and he said I must have two eggs tomorrow. “I had forgotten about eggs for breakfast.”

“I had what we English call a brisk and bracing walk.”

He looked wry. “We English! Do you count me then as a Mediterranean man?”

“No.” I could see I had committed an error. “You’re the type of dyed-in-the-wool Englishman who will never change,” I told him warmly in an attempt at reconciliation. I could not think, at the time, what provoked that ‘we English’. Later I knew it came from the resentment I had not managed to overcome. Guido, Marisa and Lucia had the father I had missed. Perhaps his lack of ease with me, I thought, only mirrored mine.

I found him later in his studio, standing back from the easel, absorbed in a partially painted picture.

"So you are doing an original." I heard the relief in my voice and hoped it had escaped him.

He half turned. "Well, yes, as I said, I do from time to time, but look at it," he said with light disdain.

"It's good. I'd be proud to have it hanging on my wall." I moved closer. The mountains were well drawn, the shadows intriguing. And he had a way with water. I could almost feel the spray.

"You're very sweet, Jane. You shall have it when it's finished."

I could see he was pleased. It will be all right, I thought. We will be friends. "Thank you," I said. "I can visualise it on my sitting room wall. It'll look just right. I haven't got many pictures. I exaggerate. I haven't got any. Can I commission you to cover my walls? There'll be no payment, of course."

He liked that. "I'll see what I can do," he said.

"Copies of old masters will be acceptable," I added, consciously stepping on dangerous ground. He didn't answer but there was still a tiny smile at the corners of his mouth. I stood looking round the studio. Propped against a wall were several folders containing canvases tied up with tape. I asked him if I could look at them.

"Sometime," he said. "I'll show you sometime." Then, changing the subject, "By the way, we've been asked to lunch."

"What a social life you lead!"

"Not really. Not at all, in fact. But we do often see my publisher."

I felt my nerves tighten. "You're lunching with the Lambardinis?"

"Yes. Would you like to come?"

"Thanks, but I hardly think so. I believe Evelina Lambardini is engaged to marry Carl." He didn't say he knew. I added, "His mother warned me off last night."

"How uncomfortable that must have been." Andrew put the palette down. "I'm so sorry."

I've only known him a few days," I said, giving all my attention to his palette, dabbing one finger in a lump of red paint. "Anyway, in the circumstances I don't think it would be very tactful of me to appear at the Lambardinis. You never know, Evelina may have found out I went to his mother's."

"Do you mind being left here alone?"

"Not at all."

"Of course you won't be entirely alone. The children will be back for a while."

I left him and wandered off down the path between the lemon trees. When I came to my room I put my bottom on the windowsill and swung my legs over. I had become adept at leaving my room this way. Donna happened to be passing the open door and saw me.

"How very athletic you are, Jane."

"You don't mind, do you? It's my short-cut. I don't think I leave any marks on the sill." I pretended to examine it carefully.

She laughed. We were so very much at ease with each other, this new stepmother and I. "Of course I don't mind," she assured me. "By the way, there was a phonecall for you. I looked for you and couldn't find you. Where were you?"

"Talking to Andrew in his studio."

"I didn't think to look there. Would you like to have lunch with Carl?"

I noted the wording. "Did he suggest it? Or you?"

"I asked him," she admitted. "How sharp you are. We're going to the Lambardinis. I thought you would like company."

So she knew I was unlikely to be welcome at the Lambardinis. She was sharp too, I echoed her in thought. I was sorely tempted to ask if this was a sudden and unexpected invitation. But did it matter? If the summons concerned me they would no doubt tell me on their return. "That would be nice," I said. "But not here. I can meet him down in the town."

Her brow puckered. "But I've already asked him here."

"I'll ring him," I said, "and tell him I'll meet him in the town."

She looked puzzled. "Maria has been informed. We have planned a nice menu for you."

"Donna," I said, warmed to the heart, "you're matchmaking. You know he's engaged to Evelina."

"Engaged?" She shrugged. "Not quite that. I think the parents would like it. But anyway, that doesn't mean he can't have lunch with you."

"I'm sorry," I said, not wanting to oppose her, but frightened witless at the though of Carl getting loose among Andrew's pictures. "I'll talk to Maria," I said. "I'll square it with her."

"No, *cara*, it is fixed up." Donna was most insistent. And a little hurt that I was opposing her.

"Really, Donna, I don't want him to come here while you're out." I was feeling desperate and trying to hide it.

"But why? The children will be here, but only for a short time. It will be nice for you to have a guest." She added kindly, "I don't like going out and leaving you alone. I want you to be happy, dear."

This, I thought, is where you tell her why Carl is in Amalfi. Why you cannot allow him to come to the villa while Andrew is out. I tried and could not get the words out. My mind was telling me that Donna, for all her warmth and undoubted kindness, had always given in to Andrew. I saw myself returning to London in disgrace, more alone in the world now than I had ever been, with the knowledge of what I might have had if things had gone differently. Two sisters. A brother. A home, a real home where I would be welcome any time I was free to come. Where I was special. I didn't want to give it up. Couldn't. Besides, if matters in Amsterdam went against Andrew, I wanted to be around. Not that I could do much to help but I could show solidarity. Offer love and loyalty. Do whatever needs doing when a man is in disgrace.

I wanted badly to make up for my mother, who had allowed another man to take her away and leave him to bear his troubles alone.

As soon as she had gone I picked up the telephone. I had the number of the Hotel Maria Convento in my head. The office put me through to his room.

"*Pronto*," that warm, Italian voice. His foreignness seemed to be to the fore now. He had been much more English on the train.

I said, "Surely you're not still in bed?"

"Not really. I've got a desk in my room. I'm working on those papers we collected last night."

I hooted. "Hanging up your laundered clothes? Listen, Carl, I don't want you to come here to lunch."

"Such charming frankness."

"You know what I mean," I said fiercely. "We could have lunch together in a restaurant."

"But I have been invited by the lady of the house and have already accepted. It would be most discourteous not to turn up."

"I'll make your excuses for you."

"See you about noon," he replied light-heartedly, and hung up.

I spent the rest of the morning down on the lido looking out on the angry sea, walking up and down in the wild wind, throwing out bits of driftwood that had been flung ashore and had fallen among the rocks, risking a ducking time and again, as though living dangerously would clear my conscience, calm my undoubted excitement, or at least show me the right way to go. I went back to the villa in time to change for lunch.

I put on my one dress. I was quite certain Donna had never owned a pair of jeans. I had begun to feel a little embarrassed about my casual gear. I dried my hair with the dryer Donna had considerately left in my room. It was stiff from the salt spray but there was no time to wash it now. I went upstairs.

The door to the study was open. I stood looking in. The old masters looked back at me. I shivered. Certainly Carl had been in here, but he had not been alone. Today it would be so easy to wander across from the salon carrying an aperitif in his hand, saying casually, "I'd like to have another look at your father's *Laughing Cavalier*." I looked round for a key. Perhaps Maria knew where it was kept. I went to the kitchen and made unlocking movements with my fingers; took her to the library and pointed to the door.

She pulled the door shut and, shaking her head as though she thought I was deranged, went back to her kitchen. Oh well, did it really matter? There were pictures hanging all over the staircase wall. I did not go out to check on the studio. Nobody in their right mind would leave a garden room unlocked.

When the doorbell rang I started forward, forgetting that in this household it was Maria's job to show guests in. I backed into the salon and stood looking out of the window, trying to assume the air of one who is accustomed to being waited on by staff, remembering how Carl had kissed me the night before, trying to still my fast beating heart.

He came into the room extending both hands. "*Ah, eccola.*"

"*Non capisco, non capisco,*" I retorted and Maria, behind him, burst into a peal of her hearty laughter. Such laughter! It seemed to fill the villa. It was she who had taught me to say, 'I do not understand.'

"How very kind of you to insist I come to lunch," he said mischievously. "It's such a terrible day. I wouldn't have known what to do with myself."

I looked into those twinkling eyes and my silly heart melted. "You know you've no right to come here," I said, trying to sound stern.

"No rights, but a genuine desire. Can I kiss you?" He moved closer.

I wanted to yell at him, You're going to marry Evelina and you're a spy! Instead, I let him take my hand. There was a sharp swish! from the other end of the room and we both swung round. Rain was sheeting against the windowpane. "That's torn it," said Carl. "Winter's here."

The doorbell rang loudly, furiously. Maria's voice echoed in the hall. There was the sound of children stampeding in out of the rain, Lucia calling: "*Mama!*" She pulled up in astonishment at the door and backed shyly away.

"Your mama is out to lunch," I said. Marisa and Guido came more quietly. I introduced them. They advanced gravely with outstretched hands. I thought how well-mannered they were. I was proud of them, my new family.

"*Buon giorno, Signor*".

"Hello, young ones." Carl was at ease with them. He called to Maria in Italian, asking if she would bring soft drinks. She must have had them ready for she hurried in with three mugs and a big glass jug of orange juice on a tray. "We're not allowed," said Lucia. "Not in the salon."

"Just this once," said Carl taking the tray from Maria with great authority. How I knew the power of that charm coupled with his natural air of authority. "You will all be very careful and not spill a drop. Especially Lucia."

He had won their hearts. They gazed at him with big eyes

as they drank the fruit juice. "We shan't be able to go back to school," Marisa said, addressing the window. "Not in that rain."

"It will be over by the time you're ready to go."

"How do you know?"

"That's what happens, doesn't it? It pours, then it stops."

"Oh, yes," said Guido, with the solemn air of one recognising a new truth.

"And tell me what you're going to do this afternoon, when the rain stops and you are back at school." Carl sat on a sofa, leaning forward, hands on his knees, giving them his full attention. I stood against the floral curtain, drinking the Martini he had poured me, watching the magic working. Lucia crept closer, leaned on his knee gazing into his face. Edged closer still. Now, with a fluid movement, one of his arms encircled her. Then she was on his knee, still gazing up at him. A lovely picture, I thought, trying to be cynical, thinking of the two Carls, trying to separate them in my mind, not succeeding.

Maria, appearing at the door, speaking to them in Italian, broke it up. Their faces fell, but the two elder ones rose obediently. "We are to have our lunch in the kitchen," Guido said, looking disconsolate. Lucia gave a little shriek of protest. Maria picked her up and firmly bore her off.

"She's a messy eater," Guido remarked matter of factly, "and she has to go to sleep, anyway. But do you think Marisa and I could have lunch with you?" He was asking me, I thought, but looking directly at Carl, involving him.

"I don't see why not," I replied. "Tell Maria we would like it." He rushed out with Marisa following and we could hear their voices raised in spirited argument.

"You've made a conquest," I said, as if he didn't always.

"I try to please."

Maria came back with Guido and Marisa, argued a little with Carl, then, with much waving of the arms and gesticulations, relented.

It was a merry lunch. Carl gave them a little wine, filling the glasses up with water. I asked him if he was sure that was allowed. They answered for me, "*Si, si,*" in chorus. "You see," he said towards the end of lunch, gesturing towards the window, "what did I tell you? The rain has stopped."

Marisa groaned.

"Bad luck," I said.

We went to the big window that looked out over the bay. The sea was laced with white foam. "I'd like to have my canoe out in that," said Guido. "Imagine!" He did ducking and diving movements, imitating a canoe on a stormy sea and provided me with the excuse I needed to get Carl out of the villa.

"Let's go down to the lido," I said. They nodded.

"I'll have to change. I won't be long." I ran downstairs, hauled my dress over my head and pulled on a cotton jumper and jeans, with sandals, and my windproof jacket. When I went back to the salon it was empty. I looked suspiciously at the closed door leading to the library. Opened it. They were not there. I asked Maria. She shrugged. Pointed to the window. Perhaps they were in the garden.

I went outside. The wind flung the door back on its hinges. I called. There was no reply. Perhaps they had gone on. I went down the steps at the side of the villa, then along the path that led to the lido. I was surprised that they should have gone without me. I hurried down the steps. The lido came into view. It was deserted. I turned back. Now I knew there was nowhere else to go but to Andrew's studio. I dashed back and took the path between the lemon trees. It was wet from the rain. I slipped on a dead leaf and nearly came down, regained my balance and went on more circumspectly. The door was open.

They were standing at the easel. I could not see the painting for it was obscured by Carl's bulk. I knew by his face, or by the stillness of him, that he had found what he was looking for.

Chapter Nine

"What are you doing here?" I demanded. My voice was shrill with fright. "Guido, you had no right to bring our guest in here. This studio is private to your father. *Privato*. You must know that."

"It's all right," protested Guido, looking upset, as well he might considering the tone I had used. "Papa lets me come in here."

"Don't blame him," said Carl. "Look here, Jane."

I did not move. Could not. He stepped aside so that I could see the picture on the easel. A half finished *Madonna and Child.*

"It's my picture," said Guido, justifying his bringing the guest here. "I was telling Signor Beaumont about Papa promising Sister Augustine a *Madonna and Child* for the *convento*. This is it. And look," Guido went on in an injured tone, "it isn't half ready and it's ages since he promised."

Carl's eyes flickered, met mine. I looked away. "Let's put it back, shall we, old chap?" He took the canvas down and slipped it into the folder that I had wanted to look at and which my father had refused to open. He bent down and tied the tape then stood up and looked gravely at me. I had not asked the subject of the Raphael portrait, but I knew, quite definitely, from his manner, that it was a *Madonna and Child.*

"I wonder why he stopped there. You'd think he'd finish a commission like that, before sending the one he was copying away. I can't help wondering if there's another one here."

I said angrily, "How many, for heaven's sake, are there? One in Bolivia. One in Amsterdam. One and a half here?"

Guido was watching us. Listening. To deflect his attention I said, "What happened to your canoe? I presume you got it safely in the boathouse?"

Guido looked dismayed. "No, I didn't. I'd better go and get it." He started for the door.

I called him back. "You've left it in the grotto?" He nodded. "You can't go in there with this sea running," I said.

"I have to," he shouted over his shoulder as he fled out of the door. "It'll get broken up!"

I rushed after him along the slippery path. "Guido, stop!" I yelled. I had to slow down for a little way but where the leaf-strewn path came out into the open I put on speed, rounded the corner of the lower wall of the villa where my room lay and sped up the steps. "Guido! Guido!" I shouted. "Stop!" He had disappeared from sight. When I came round the back of the building where the path ran parallel to the road I saw him again. He was going through the gate. I kept running. "Guido, stop!" I shouted again. I didn't doubt my ability to control a nine-year-old but I had to catch him first.

I slipped and slithered along the wet path, then headed down the steps. He was gaining ground from me. If either of us fell, there were only the vicious cactus plants to break what would be a precipitous descent. "Guido!" I shouted again. He continued to ignore me. I was frightened. I had a picture in my mind of the narrow shelf that ran along the side of the grotto which could only be used with care even when the stone was dry.

He had reached the boulders. I hurtled after him and at last caught up for he had stopped and was looking in consternation at the water swirling up round the rocks. There was no question of getting near the grotto. He stood there looking devastated, his hands hanging by his sides, while the sea rose up outside the mouth and funnelled into the grotto, roaring. White spray flew high in the air, as high as the mouth. He turned to me with tears on his cheeks. "It will be broken up," he sobbed. "My canoe!"

I put an arm round him and turned to look at the churning sea. There was no sign of it. But then, I thought, if it had been washed out it would have been splintered against the rocks. "How far did you take it into the cave?" I asked.

His face crumpled. "Not very far. We didn't think there would be a storm."

I held him against me, comforting him. It was practically windless here in the shelter of the rocks and the cliff. The power of the waves came from the ocean itself. We watched it gather itself up a hundred yards out then rage in, crashing up against the cliff, funnelling in to the grotto. We were mesmerised by its sheer force, the beauty of it, and its danger.

"Hell's teeth!"

I looked round. Carl was standing close by, hands on hips, surveying the scene. He said comfortingly, "It'll calm down after a while. You've got to go back to school, young man. Tell me exactly where the canoe is, and I'll go in after it when I can."

I opened my mouth to say I thought it would be foolhardy to attempt to go in possibly for twenty-four hours, then closed it again. Guido needed something to cling to. We told Carl about the ledge that ran along the wall from the entrance to the grotto.

"How long?"

"Maybe a hundred yards. Probably less." Possibly a lot less, I thought. It isn't easy to judge how far you are walking when you're going slowly and your eyes are on your feet all the way. I didn't say it was no great distance. I didn't want to give him the impression it would be easy.

"You'd better go back to school, Guido," he said. "Maybe I'll have the canoe out by the time you get home. Don't count on it, though."

Guido asked, "Can you swim?"

"Oh yes, but I wouldn't want to go into that."

We made our way back up the cliff path and crossed to the villa. Guido was late for school now. Marisa had already gone. I found his coat and buttoned him into it. He sped off. Maria was singing over the clattering of dishes in the kitchen.

Carl, who had been looking out of the window, turned. "Jane, we've got to go back to the studio."

"I think you'd better leave," I said. "You had no right to go there in the first place."

"Guido wanted to show me the picture his father was painting for the nuns. How could I turn him down? He's only a little boy."

"He's not that little," I said angrily. "Where did you get the key?"

"He knew where it was. Under a stone near the door."

I couldn't believe that Andrew should keep the key to his studio under a stone near the door. But perhaps I ought to. He had a poor opinion of his own paintings.

"Come on," Carl said in that warm, persuasive way he had of twisting me round his little finger, "He's not doing that Madonna from memory. There's got to be another one there."

"In a studio the key to which is kept outside the door under a stone?" But it was too late to chase him away. He had a story of sorts and it was one that could do untold harm. I made a conscious decision to go and look through Andrew's folios. For better or worse, I thought, I'm in this up to my neck.

"Yes, all right," I said. "Anyway, we've got to go back to lock up."

He didn't say he had done that but as we went along the path between the lemon trees he bent down and picked the key up. Nobody in their right mind, I thought, was going to keep a picture worth a fortune in a garden studio so casually locked that a child could lay his hands on the key. I felt better for recognising that. I said as he unlocked the door, "Plenty of artists copy old masters."

"Do they?"

"If he, by some curious chance, stumbled on the genuine Madonna and decided to sell it, why shouldn't he make one copy for the nuns and one for himself?"

"You're assuming the South American collector has a fake? You've got to remember this chap."

"Of course. I hope so."

He unlocked the door and put the key in his pocket. I felt sick with apprehension. It was like clinging to a cliff, wanting to fall and get the horror over with.

Carl picked up a folio. "You look through that," he said. "That's where the half finished copy is." He reached up and brought down another from the shelf above. "I'll take this one."

I came across the half finished portrait immediately, took it out and put it on the easel. Then I went through the rest of the canvases. We worked in feverish haste, scarcely noting the subjects except for the fact that each one was not a *Madonna and Child*. I found it, sandwiched in between two sheets of brown paper, as though Andrew had made a half-hearted attempt to hide it. I took it out and placed it beside the half finished picture on the easel. "There it is," I said. "Now, what does it prove?"

He looked at it hard, as though he really did know something about pictures. "You aren't by any chance working for the people in Amsterdam who are selling the picture, are you?" I asked, my voice sharp with fear.

"No."

I knew now that Carl didn't lie. He teased when he didn't want to answer, but he didn't lie. We put the canvases back where we had found them, went out and locked the door. "You seemed to recognise the picture," I said. "Is this the one that's for sale?"

"I couldn't be sure. I've only seen a newspaper picture of it, but I think so. Raphael did a series of paintings of the Madonna and Child."

"Where are they? Are they all accounted for?"

"Of the three that are best known there's one in Dresden and two in Florence."

"Is it one of those?"

"No."

"You know them, then?"

He nodded.

"You do know about art?"

"A bit." He bent down to put the key under the stone.

"And you haven't seen that Madonna before?"

"No." He straightened.

"So, what are you going to do now?"

"Make myself scarce," he said. "I hear voices. Thank you for lunch."

"What are you going to do?" I hissed.

He shrugged. "Take myself for a walk. Think." He took my hands in his in that way he had and kissed me on the cheek, then went swifly round the corner of the villa and disappeared in the garden. I returned to my room the usual way, by the window, and flopped down on my bed. I didn't know where I was now. I was riddled with guilt. I had violated Andrew's privacy and found out nothing.

But it was too late for regrets. We had done what we had done. I simply did not believe my father was a swindler. I would stake my life on it. I wanted this matter cleared up, his good name, lost so long ago, reinstated. I wanted for him what my mother and stepfather had taken away. Donna had created a little paradise here at the Villa Passerina which was all very well. These two unworldly people in their perfect marriage were bad for each other. Someone had to shoot a thunderbolt through the place. I saw myself as that thunderbolt.

Through the open door I could hear my father and stepmother's conversation drifting down the stairs. Then Andrew called, "Jane, are you down there?" He sounded grave.

"Yes." I went slowly to meet him, readying myself.

He was standing by the open door that led into his library. "Come in," he said. He did not smile at me.

I thought with a great surge of relief that I was not going to have to tell him I had brought an enemy into his camp. The Lambardinis had told him for me! Andrew seated himself behind the big desk. He indicated that I take a high-backed leather one that stood in the corner.

"I'll come straight to the point and get it over with," Andrew said. "The Lambardinis invited us to lunch today specifically to ask me to stop you seeing Carl Beaumont."

"Oh," I said.

"Is that all?" He gave me a quizzical look.

I was breathless. Thrown off balance. I felt more shock than relief.

"You've only known him a short time."

"Yes."

"You didn't know he was the property of their daughter?"

"Yes – er—" The property of their daughter! That was putting it pretty strongly, I thought. Or was Andrew teasing? I looked into his eyes and saw they were smiling.

"There, that's all over," he said. "It's none of my business. But Antonio and I are good friends, and since I have been asked to say this, I have done it. No hard feelings?"

"No hard feelings," I replied truthfully. As he said, he was only doing what he had been asked to do.

"I gather Signora Beaumont is very rich. The Lambardinis would like their daughter to marry well."

"Most parents do," I said.

"I suppose so." Andrew adjusted some papers on his desk. "Now, let's get on to more pleasant and less personal topics." He looked up, smiling.

I had my moment. I took a deep breath, but instead of speaking, let it out again. He could see I had something to say. He waited, wearing that quizzical look I was coming to know. I said in a rush, "Today Guido showed me a half-finished picture you are painting for the nuns. Is it a copy of the Raphael that's for sale in Amsterdam? The one the reporters are bothering you about? Did it come from you?"

He wiped a hand across his brow.

I said, rather desperately, "I'm sorry, Andrew, but I have to know. I'm terribly sorry to put you on the spot like this, but . . . I'm your daughter, not your wife. And I don't know you. And I'm accustomed to people being straightforward. Why can't you talk about this? What are you hiding?"

With his elbows on the desk he rubbed his fingertips up and down his forehead and uttered a leaden sigh. "Yes," he said, "I had begun to do a copy for them."

"And the one that's for sale? You put it up?"

"Yes, my dear. I am sorry this business should have come up just when we found each other, but there it is. Life takes some strange turns."

I leaned forward in my seat. "Go on, Andrew. You have to talk to me. Is it real, this picture? I mean, is it a genuine Raphael?"

"I believe so."

"Then why don't you come out in the open?"

"Because if it isn't genuine then the whole ghastly business is going to blow up again."

"But it has blown up, Andrew. You must accept it. It has blown up and it's being fuelled by your silence."

"I'm waiting to hear. Marking time," he said.

"Where did you get the picture?" I felt guilty asking that question, knowing he had got it from Evelina.

"I was offered it about eighteen months ago. I thought it a very good copy and paid the owner accordingly."

"How much?"

He looked at me oddly. "About a million and a quarter lire."

"How much is that?"

He thought for a moment. "Around five hundred pounds."

"You bought it for your own collection?"

"Yes and no. One deals from time to time." He looked down at the backs of his hands that were splayed out on the desk. "Donna and I had a trip to Florence about six months ago. We went to the Pitti Palace – one always does. And the Uffizi. That's what an artist goes to Florence for, to see the art galleries. They have the *Madonna del Gran Duca*. I'd seen it often enough before, of course. But never to compare it with a copy." Andrew's face softened. He looked up at me. "There's a divine tenderness in the faces of Raphael's Madonnas that it's impossible to recreate. No one ever has. I came home convinced mine was authentic."

He looked up as though he wanted to check on my expression. Then down again at his hands.

"So I made a copy for myself – quite a poor one I have to say. I would never fool myself into thinking I could copy the look Raphael got. I'll show it to you. It's in my studio."

I was glad he was not looking at me at that moment.

"It's like comparing diamonds with glass, or gold with a base metal," he said. "Then I began another, but I haven't finished it. I think I'll give the first copy to the *convento* if they still want it. I don't want to do it twice. I lost interest, copying from my poor copy."

"Did you tell the dealer in Amsterdam you thought it was authentic?" I held my breath.

"No, I merely suggested they examine it very carefully. This chap I sent it to considers himself to be an expert on the period. He telephoned to say he reckoned it was an original. I told him not to stick his neck out until he had a few more experts examine it. But you know how people talk. He had to tell a few friends. And when there's a new find like this in the art world, news travels like wild fire.

"He happened to have a Director of the National Gallery over at the time," Andrew went on, "and showed it to him. That is how the offer to buy it came about – somewhat prematurely, I thought. I specifically asked him to keep my name out of it, but no one can ever resist dropping hints. And you know what newspapers are. The rest is muck-stirring.

"This Bolivian came up with the fact that he had the original, sold to him by a Los Angeles art dealer not long ago for a very large sum. I decided the most sensible thing to do was to lie low for a bit. It can't take long to sort out. I suppose this chap in South America will have to send his picture over. If he gets irate enough, he will. Meanwhile, I will not talk to reporters. I will not have them here!"

I swallowed convulsively. "What will the picture be worth, if it is genuine?"

Andrew said, "Who knows! These old masters have reached ridiculous heights now, haven't they?"

"Andrew," I said, tracing a finger along the polished wood of the desk, not looking at him, "if this picture does prove to be genuine, what would you do about the person who sold it to you?"

"What do you mean?"

"I mean, you only gave her five hundred pounds."

"Her?" repeated Andrew, frowning. "It came from a chap called Frattuni. I don't even know him. But yes, if I have mistakenly undervalued the picture, I would feel morally obliged to give this man something."

He eyed me consideringly, with faint suspicion. "Why did you say 'she'?"

"I thought you bought it from Evelina," I said boldly. I had to be bold if I was to get to the bottom of this.

"Did she tell you that?"

"I am afraid I was eavesdropping. She was here one day. I overheard you talking. I tackled her about it. She tried to stop me telling Carl she had a connection with the picture. Why doesn't she want Carl to know?"

"I am not aware she doesn't want him to know," Andrew replied. "I knew nothing of the young man until you brought him here. Perhaps she makes a business of selling pictures and taking commission. She might not want it known generally."

"Who is Frattuni?"

"I've no idea. She didn't seem to want me to know that. I didn't pursue the subject, since at the time I did not consider the picture to be of any importance."

We sat in silence for a while. Then: "Andrew," I began hesitantly, "that partner of yours who committed suicide—"

"Is dead," he broke in firmly.

"No, please. You must tell me."

He looked across the desk at me, those straight blue eyes a little stern. "Donna has never felt the need to ask."

"She is your wife. She is in love with you. It's different. I am a stranger, and yet, I am so closely connected. It is important to me to know what happened." I said it beseechingly.

He was silent for a little time. Then, "All right," he replied, "if that is how you feel. I did not paint those forgeries for which I went to court. You may have my solemn word on that, if it's what you want. And nor did I offer them for sale knowing them to be forged."

I nodded. I believed him, absolutely. I felt I was getting to know him. He was a man who had difficulty dealing with people, facing the world. A loser, perhaps, let down by a very human and not very strong woman, saved by an angel. An Italian angel with a heart of gold. But Donna the angel didn't have her feet on the ground. I did.

"I know you don't want me to talk about this," I said. "You've made it clear. But I didn't know your partner. I've come into your life in a very unusual fashion. You must meet me halfway." His eyes were wary. "You must, Andrew," I insisted. "You really must. Howard told me about your partner committing suicide. Forgive me if I sound a little blunt, but I find it hard to believe that a man would kill himself just to avoid a trial from which he expected to be acquitted."

Andrew's head came up. His hands were still outspread on the desk. He stared at the ceiling. His face was grave. "When one goes for trial one does not *expect* to be acquitted," he explained, his voice a little strained. "One hopes, Jane. Hopes," he repeated. "And a dying man, you must realise, has already given up."

"Your partner was guilty, wasn't he?" I asked softly.

"You are young, my dear, and you have a lot to learn about people, and about life."

I was sitting up straight in the chair now, angry in defence of my father, whom I felt to be confused by the wrong values. "I don't think you're being fair to Donna and the children," I told him. "I don't think you should have this thing hanging over you."

He looked wry. "Are you going to wave a magic wand?"

"Something like that." I was feeling good when I left him. He needed me. It was something I had not experienced before, someone needing me. I decided to talk to Carl and ask him to help. He was going to get some sort of a story. Perhaps I would be able to deflect him so that his story took the limelight from Andrew. I thought it should not be beyond my ability to run this Frattuni to ground.

I went to my room and telephoned him at the Hotel Maria Convento. He was not in, the desk clerk informed me. I told him who I was. "Yes, yes," he replied. He knew my voice. I don't suppose there were too many English visitors at this time of year. "He went out to lunch and has not come back."

I left a message for him to ring me when he returned, then wandered out into the garden. The air was still. I heard the children come home. They were always noisy on arrival as though coming home was a celebration.

Wanting to be on my own for a while to think I walked down to the lido. The sea was calmer. The high water mark showed that it had receded some distance down the sand. I wondered if Carl would return later to check out Guido's canoe. I felt he was the kind of man who would honour a promise to a child. I stood looking pensively out over the bay. Frattuni. If Carl had no knowledge of him then I was going to have to ask Evelina. That would be unfortunate, I conceded, but I was prepared to do it.

When I returned to the villa everyone was looking for Guido. "So you were down at the lido? He wasn't there?" Donna asked, looking worried.

"No."

"He came home with the girls," she said, "then disappeared. We thought he must be with you."

I said, "I think I know where he may have gone." I told them he had been worried about his canoe. "I'll run down to the grotto. He shouldn't be there on his own."

I sped up the steps to the back of the villa then across to the gate leading into the wasteland. The path was still wet from the morning rain, and slippery. I walked swiftly, though carefully. The steps were slippery, too. I didn't for one moment think Guido would attempt to go into the grotto so I wasn't really worried. The water was wilder here than on the lido, being trapped by the two small headlands. When I looked up I saw Guido standing alone a few yards from the entrance to the grotto, hands in pockets, shoulders hunched. Then I saw he had a man-sized jacket draped over his narrow shoulders.

"Guido!" I cried, my voice shrill with anxiety. He heard me and ran to meet me. I couldn't take my eyes off the jacket.

His small face was taut with fear. "Carl's in the grotto. He went to see if my canoe's still there. Ages ago. He hasn't come out."

I looked at the spray-covered rocks that marked the edge of the grotto where the cliff rose behind. An enormous wave thundered forward, swept inside with a terrifying roar, then the ocean sucked it out again. "How could he go in?" I shouted over the noise of the water.

"He waited and waited." Guido's words tumbled over each other in his distress. "It was quieter for a while. Like now, you see. It's quiet."

I saw what he meant. The ocean could hold the surge. It was holding now, building up, getting ready to rush in again. That's what I was seeing. It was getting ready to let go.

"He counted the big waves and the small waves. He did it for a long time. He said there's a rhythm. What's that?"

I explained.

"So when the sea went flat, he dashed in. He said he'd see if the canoe was there and take it further up the cave if he had to, and come out when it went flat again. But it hasn't gone flat. Not like that. Not like when he went in. Doesn't seem to have," said Guido, looking uncertain. "Anyway, he hasn't come out."

I thought it was one thing to gauge an entrance, quite another to do it in reverse. I was rigid with fear. "I expect he knows how to get out," I said, not believing it, wondering if I should dash for help. But surely Carl wouldn't do anything foolish! A man does not give his life for a boy's canoe. But he could lose it having an adventure. That was what frightened me. I could imagine Carl, high on the challenge, racing the tide. I scanned the water again. He was a strong swimmer, that I knew, but the strongest swimmer was unlikely to have the strength to grapple with this surge of water. He could be thrown up against the rocks, hit his head . . .

I swung round. "I'm going for help."

"Shall I wait here, or come with you?"

He looked pathetic standing there, white-faced, with Carl's

jacket over his shoulders, enormous on his narrow boy's figure. I said, "I think you had better stay. Don't on any account go near the water. Just watch." I couldn't bear to say aloud what he was watching for. He knew. He nodded and I hurried back to the steps. Just as I was about to go out of sight behind the rocks I shouted, "You won't move, will you?"

He shook his head. I climbed at a run to begin with, then lost my breath and had to slow. My legs were puttyish with fear. At the top I sped along the path towards the villa. Inevitably, I slipped and sprawled on my back, picked myself up and ran on, then fell over again. I was half-crying when I burst in at the door. Andrew was standing in the hallway. He advanced towards me, exclaiming. "Jane! What on earth—" Donna and the girls came running.

With what breath I had left I told them. "Ring someone," I said. They were starting at me in astonishment. "Coastguards, or whatever you have here. Ring someone," I repeated distractedly.

"If he got in, then he's perfectly safe," Andrew said. "That cave slopes upwards into the cliff. "But how do you know—" He broke off.

"We don't know." I felt my face crumpling. "He could have been washed out. Guido wouldn't necessarily see. Please," I begged Andrew, "ring whoever . . . whoever . . ." I couldn't go on.

He went to the telephone. Donna put her arms round me. "And what about Guido?" Andrew asked as he dialled.

"I'll go back," I said. "I'm sure he will be sensible, but he's frightened."

Andrew had gone into a flood of Italian. I understood only *carabinieri*. Police.

Marisa said she would accompany me. Maria had come out of the kitchen to see what the excitement was about. She hurled some orders at Marisa and stalked off, then came back with coats for both girls. I dashed out of the door. Behind me I heard Marisa call, "Wait for me!" There was no time. I sped up the steps to the back of the villa then across the garden and through the gate. The path was still muddy. I slipped and slid as I ran, lost my balance twice. I tried to take the steps slowly and with care but not succeeding, fell. A jutting rock broke my fall, painfully. I staggered to my feet clutching sore ribs and continued, fretting at my inability to move faster.

Chapter Ten

Guido was standing where I had left him. "It's all right," I said, not believing it was all right at all.

The waves are flattening out," Guido said. They were still sweeping into the grotto but they no longer struck the cliff at either side. "It's getting calmer. I'm sure it is." His little face had brightened.

"Yes. I believe it is. How flat was it when he went in? As flat as this?"

"I can't remember."

There were voices and we turned to see Marisa picking her way towards us with Andrew coming behind. He said as he approached, "They're sending a boat out." He eyed the entrance to the grotto and remarked, "It would take a mighty big tide to get right into the cave." He seemed to be saying Carl was bound to be safe. I thought afterwards: This is how he is. He thinks nothing will happen because he doesn't want it to. This is how he lives. But it didn't occur to me at the time. I was frightened out of my wits.

"Carl doesn't strike me as a fool," he said. "I'm sure he wouldn't have gone in if he didn't think he could make it. He's probably twiddling his thumbs in the cave now. Prepared to sit there until it's perfectly safe to come out. That's what I would do."

"He must know Guido would be worried."

"I dare say he credits Guido with enough sense to let us know, and us with enough sense not to come after him." I could have reminded him Guido had not rushed back to the villa to inform us. That he had stayed here, a possible danger to himself, until I came. What was the point? I thought, he doesn't face up to things. This is how he is. Don't recognise it, that's his philosophy, and it won't happen.

More voices. We turned. Donna and Lucia emerged from behind the rocks, holding hands. The sun, already close to the horizon, had gone behind the clouds. We heard the roar of a boat's engine and a moment later saw it in the fading light, speeding round the headland. We stood in silence, watching as it sped up and down. Guido pointed to something dark lifting above the water. We held our breaths. It ran in closer. It was some sort of tin, or drum. Our collective breaths ran out again.

"Guido, go back and get my big torch." That was Andrew.

Guido didn't want to go. And nor did I. Donna said placidly, "I will go. Lucia, come with me." They disappeared into the gloom. Another boat came roaring across the water. And a moment later, another. The three of them criss-crossed the bay in formation. I shivered. I found myself remembering being held down in the school baths by a bigger girl. The feeling of my chest bursting as I fought for breath, my mouth and ears filled with water. And this was salt. So much more harsh. Why am I thinking like this? I asked myself distractedly. He is safe, high up in the cave. Andrew says he is. Andrew knows.

We watched the lights speeding across the water that was dark sapphire now, nearly black. I felt the beginning of tears at the back of my throat, the forewarning lump. Such a short time I had known Carl, and yet there was all this passion in me. It could have been so wonderful, if he had not been a threat to my father. If he had not got drowned trying to find a child's canoe. I wondered why he should risk his life for such a small thing, then thought, he was a boy once. Perhaps he lost something and remembers the pain. I recognised I was raising him to sainthood. My feelings were getting out of hand.

Donna arrived back alone, carrying the torch. Andrew took it from her and moved towards the mouth of the grotto. I opened my mouth to say, don't go in, then saw Donna standing motionless, her face calm. I thought, she not only trusts Andrew, she trusts. Just trusts. That is why she has so much to give. She doesn't tear herself to pieces like the rest of us.

It was nearly dark, now. Andrew had stopped at the grotto mouth. He shone the torch inside. The water was lively but no longer threatening. It lapped around his legs. A wave bigger than the rest gathered itself up, surged over the hollow it had formed in rising and crashed into the grotto. Andrew leapt back.

Guido said again, "He counted. They get smaller after a while."

I began to count. The black water rose, then sank. It rose again, came in forcefully, swept back. The next wave was less powerful. And the next. I could see how the pattern changed. Again, Andrew shone the torch inside the grotto. It was no use shouting. Carl would not hear over the sound of the water, but he might see the light and know we were here. He switched the torch off and came to join us. "Why don't you go up? I'll wait."

None of us moved.

"It could take hours for the water to calm sufficiently for him to risk coming out," Andrew said. My mind latched on to the word risk. Carl had risked going in. He was a man who took risks. I wanted to be there when he risked coming out, though not knowing what I could do to help. It was the not knowing that held me there. Held us all. Going back to the comfort of the villa was a kind of abandonment.

After a while we heard voices. There was bobbing torchlight on the cliff path. A few minutes later men emerged from the darkness of the rocks. They spoke to Andrew in Italian.

"What are they saying?"

Donna answered, "They're not too worried. They say if he's sensible and doesn't try to come out—"

"If he's in there." My voice trembled.

"Of course. He was foolish to go in. That's what they're saying." She spoke indulgently, "But he is young and strong. Young men do these things. It is their need to prove to themselves they are men."

"And it may be to please others," I said defensively. "Guido was upset about his canoe."

"Of course." She put an arm round me. "It was very kind of him."

The Italians voiced their opinions with a good deal of arm-waving. They laughed. Expressed their feelings with the ubiquitous Italian shrug. It was dark now. I was beginning to feel cold. "What do they say?"

Andrew translated. "There's nothing they can do. It has happened before. There has not been a fatality – yet. And as they say, there's no point in our staying here. Carl wouldn't be so foolish as to try to get out until daylight. The sea should be a good deal calmer by then. Come on, Jane." His tone made the request into an order. Guido had dropped Carl's jacket on the ground. I picked it up and folded it over my arm. We trailed back up the cliff face.

"It's not as though he'll be cold," Andrew said as we paused to get our breath. "The temperature in these caves scarcely varies. Even if he got a bit wet going in he'll be quite comfortable." He paused, then, "Silly ass," he muttered.

Guido said indignantly, "Carl is not a silly ass. He's a kind man. He went to save my canoe."

"Yes, well," said Andrew. "A canoe. That's what I meant. It's only a canoe, when all's said and done."

"It's *my* canoe," shouted Guido, close to tears. He jumped down two steps and flailed his father with his fists. Andrew picked him up, slung him over his shoulder. "You're a bit of a weight to cart up here, but it's one way of controlling you," he said tersely. I could see he was out of sorts. Was he annoyed at Carl? Or was he more worried than he would admit? Upside down, with his face in his father's back, Guido begged to be released. Donna, coming behind, ruffled his hair. "You are lucky to get a ride," she said, laughing.

We trudged on up in the darkness, then made our way along the slippery track that ran across the wasteland. At the gate Andrew released Guido. He and Marisa sped through and across the garden. Maria had put the lights on and the door was open. We took off our muddy shoes and trailed in. Lucia heard us and came running upstairs in her pyjamas, shouting in Italian. I picked out Carl's name.

I will have to put my mind to studying the language seriously, I thought. In moments of excitement people don't remember. I laid Carl's jacket over the banister and went downstairs to get a clean pair of sandals and tidy myself up. I felt desolate. They were taking it all so calmly. What if he hadn't made it? What if he had been caught by one of those great surges while running along the ledge?

But hadn't Guido said the water was flat when he went in? If that was so, he wouldn't have been caught. I brushed my hair, surprised to find it was damp, as was my jumper. I found a clean T-shirt and put it on. My jeans were damp also but they would dry. I had better ask about washing.

Spicy scents from the kitchen drifted down the stairs. Maria, preparing a meal. In the cave Carl would have nothing to eat. I didn't want supper. I felt too vulnerable to go upstairs and face my father, who thought Carl a silly ass for trying to help a child. I wanted to cry about it. About the fact that now that I was away from the grotto, Carl might be floating face downwards in the bay.

Was that what the police had been saying? 'He has probably been swept out to sea. You had better go home and we will see to it in the morning.' This was the trouble with not knowing the language. But would they have said such things in front of Marisa and Guido? No. The tranquillity of the villa folded itself around me. I must go back upstairs. At such times one should endeavour not to be alone.

Andrew and I met at the door to the salon. He smiled at me. Squeezed my arm. Lucia was sitting on the floor in the middle of the room carefully arranging little plastic cards in a row. There was a leather wallet lying on the carpet beside her. Andrew said, "What's that, Lucia? Where did you get my wallet?" He bent down to pick it up. Lucia swept the cards together, protesting that they were hers, she had found them. "Come on now, darling," coaxed Andrew, holding out his hand. "Give them to me."

"No." She jumped to her feet. Held them behind her back.

Andrew swept her up in his arms. The cards scattered across the floor. I swiftly collected them and handed them to him. He put the child down, opened the wallet and, as he was about to slid the cards in, he paused. Frowned. "What's this?"

He looked up, straight at me. His face that had been so serene a moment ago was livid. "Southern European News Service!"

My mind blanked out with shock. After a while, it seemed like hours, I remembered how I had carelessly laid Carl's jacket across the banister where anything might have fallen out of a pocket. "It's Carl's wallet," I managed.

"I will give it to Carl," said Lucia. "Give to me. Where's Carl?"

Andrew had not taken his eyes off me. "You brought him here! You!" He stood very tall, very lean and quite formidable with his hands on his hips, looking at me as though he loathed me.

"I'm sorry," I whispered. "I'm so terribly sorry. I couldn't be more sorry, Andrew."

"*You*, my own daughter."

I burst into tears.

Donna came running. She put her arms round me. "What is it? What has happened, darling?"

"Carl," said Andrew angrily, "is a reporter. My own daughter brought a reporter into my house! My daughter!" He put the wallet and the cards down on a small table as though they burnt his hand.

"You have no right to say that," flared Donna, a new and passionate Donna whom I scarcely recognised. "I am sorry to have to mention it, darling, but Jane does not owe you the loyalty of a daughter." Then to me, gently, "Your father does not mean to be unkind."

"So this is your revenge, is it?" Andrew ignored his wife. Without waiting for a reply he added, "You can leave any time you like." He stalked out of the room. We heard the library door slam. Lucia, uttering a prolonged wail, flung herself face downwards on the floor. Maria rushed in, swept her up and tactfully disappeared. Donna gave me a quick kiss. "It will be all right," she said. "I will talk to him." She went with swift footsteps out of the room and crossed the passage. I snatched up the wallet, shoved the cards inside and made for the stairs. Behind me she flung open the library door.

"Andrew!" I stopped dead on the first step, riveted by her flooding anger. "You will not do this to Jane," she was saying. "You will not. She has come to replace Leslie whom you took away from me. To send him to your English school!" She spat the words at him. "Your English school!" she repeated. "As if that was something worth having! You knew I didn't want him to go but you sent him anyway. And we lost him. Now, Jane has come to us. A precious gift in exchange for my beloved son. You will not get rid of her. I will see to that."

"You're being silly, Donna."

"Is it silly to love your own flesh and blood? Jane is that."

"Not yours," he said. His voice rose, angry and despairing. "Oh God, is there no end to the bad luck that comes from England!"

"Your bad luck does not come from England," snapped Donna, her voice chill. "You didn't deal with your problems in England and so they followed you. And they will follow you until you do deal with them."

I pulled Carl's jacket off the banister rail, crept down the stairs to my room and closed the door carefully. My bag was under the bed. I pulled it out and hastily threw the few clothes I had into it, higgledy-piggledy, then laid Carl's jacket and his wallet on top of them. I didn't stop to ask myself if this was the sensible thing to do. My head was full of the fact that I had seen the canker in the apple of my father's perfect marriage, and I had to get out before any more harm was done.

I trudged grimly down the road with my bag. Paused for a rest. Changed the bag over to my other hand. Any moment now, I thought, they will come after me and I will be humiliated. Reduced to the status of a wilful child, running away.

I felt the pain of what I had done like a personal wound. I had no rights here in this foreign land. I had been born to Howard and Margaret Knight of Highgate, London. If the circumstances of my birth were quixotic, it was my doom and my destiny to be their daughter for better or worse. When your father has abandoned you, and you seek him out and smash up his hard-won happiness, he has every right to say, as Andrew did, 'So this is your revenge!' I shivered.

No one came after me. The fact that I wasn't worth pursuing was equally an insult and a relief. Perhaps they were still arguing about the rightness of my going. 'Our marriage is more important than a girl we don't even know. A blood relation, yes, but what is blood? We do not know her. We have taken in a stranger and these are the consequences. Disruption. Publicity that could do the family (the real family) untold harm.' Donna would no doubt in the end give way to Andrew as she had always done.

I came to the bottom of the hill and paused. Both arms were aching now. Where were the taxis? Perhaps I would find one on the front. I picked up my bag again. Trudged on, down the narrow street that led to the beach. Pause. Change arms. Great blankets of seaweed, driftwood and discoloured foam swung up with the tide. Fragments lay discarded untidily on the sand as the water receded.

I trudged across the front for there were no taxis down here, either. I came to the foot of the ridge where the road wound up and out of the town. It was from this road the steps erupted and led to the hotel. I saw the task of getting there with my bag as insuperable. I sat down on a low wall waiting for some strength to return.

A woman went past carrying a heavy basket. I watched her make for a flight of steps that swung away to the left. These mountain people with their short, sturdy legs were built to deal with their environment. They had been going up and down carrying their burdens since childhood. I lifted my bag and set out again. My spirits had reached a very low ebb. My suitcase might have been packed with stones. I lifted it despondently from one step to the next. Another step. Another. If you keep on you have to get there in the end.

I did. I sat down on the ledge that had been fashioned out of the mountainside to make the hotel car park, and leaned back against the retaining wall. Emotion and the long climb, relief at having made it, had taken my final reserves. Another forty or fifty steps to go. They could wait. I closed my eyes.

A patter of footsteps. One of the boys who worked around the hotel was standing looking down at me. He pointed to the bag, flooded me with round Italian vowels.

"*Si*, *si*," I replied gratefully.

He picked it up. It wasn't heavy to him. How could it be? A pair of jeans, a skirt, a dress, a T-shirt or two, shoes. Essentials only. He swung off up the steep incline and I trudged after him.

The manager was behind the desk, looking concerned at what the boy was relating. "What has happened?" He came forward as I trudged over the threshold.

"I need a room for the night," I said.

"No problem. Your room is still vacant. The same one. There are no new guests. The season—" He gestured that it was over, more or less. "But what has happened?"

I couldn't answer. I was having trouble with my emotions. He tried again. "Signor Beaumont is not here. You have walked?" He could see I had not stepped out of a taxi. The boy picked up my bag and went off up the narrow carpeted stairs.

"Yes," I managed. "I walked."

"Sit down over there," he said, pointing towards the inner courtyard that opened off the foyer. "I will bring you a drink."

There was no one around. I went in and sat down. Moments later he returned carrying two bulbous glasses. "Brandy," he said. He pulled out the chair opposite. "Something is wrong, Signorina?"

I took a sip of the brandy before replying. It burned my throat. I took another sip. I told him about Carl going into the grotto.

"Ah! The grotto." He shook his head, smiling. "There is often persons stuck in that grotto," he said. "No, not often. But it does happen, once in a while. It is safe enough, so long as they do not try to get out until the sea is calm."

"The police came."

"*Si, si*. They would. But not worry for a man. Children, that is different. No one has drowned there. You see, the water does not go right up into the cave. There is a corner—" He proceeded to demonstrate with a finger on the table top. "The ledge ends at this corner where is the cave." I nodded. "The wave go up straight ahead." His finger pursued an imaginary line beyond the little promontory where Guido had taken his canoe out when Lucia and I were with him. "It don't go much into the cave."

"Thank you, Signor Vallini." I smiled at him.

"Luigi," he said.

"Luigi." The brandy was already working. It occurred to me that Andrew might have explained the cave like this to me, then I realised I was being unfair. This man knew the area from boyhood. Andrew did not.

"He is all right," said Luigi earnestly.

"Yes. I do see." I nodded, feeling comforted.

"Come. Drink up your brandy. You will need to have some dinner, too."

"Yes." I allowed myself to be taken over.

"He do not have to go along the wet ledge," Luigi went on. "It will be slippery. He can come out in the canoe when it is safe."

"Yes. Yes, of course." With the help of the brandy he was

convincing me. But his 'when it is safe' struck a wrong chord. Would a man of Carl's temperament wait until it was safe? There was boredom to consider. And a young man's sense of adventure.

"I will bring you another aperitif?"

"I'd better not. Thank you. You've been very kind."

"Kind?" He shrugged in that Italian way. "It is nothing. I will bring you the menu. You will be able to eat a good meal because there is nothing to worry about."

"Yes."

"And in the morning, I think Signor Beaumont will be back here. I have heard the weather report," he said. "Tomorrow is sunshine. All sunshine. So the sea will be calm again." Again that funny little Italian shrug. "It does not hurt a man to spend a night underground where it is anyway warm. You want the menu now?"

I said I would go to my room and tidy up. My legs were working again. The brandy had given me strength. I went up the narrow stairs with a lighter heart.

It took a little time to sort out the mess in my suitcase. I shook out Carl's jacket, held its English tweed to my cheek and sent up a little prayer that he should be safe. Then I hung it in my wardrobe and put his wallet in my handbag. I put my own clothes on hangers. I didn't feel like dressing up but I couldn't have dinner in damp jeans and a T-shirt. I put on the yellow blouse and skirt. My sandals were damp. I slipped into the one pair of shoes I had brought.

There were now two couples in the little courtyard. It looked very pretty with the candles on the tables flaring. I went in and sat down. A waiter brought me a carafe of red wine. I indicated that I did not want it. He cast a worried look towards the open door. "Signor Vallini send," he said.

I allowed him to fill my glass.

It was when I was nearly through my meal that I became aware of the light. Diners at the other tables were looking up at the sky. An enormous moon, round as a ball, had come up over the mountain and was shining directly into the courtyard. It reflected back from the white walls, bathing the courtyard in an eerie sort of daylight. The people around exclaimed with surprise.

A woman at the next table included me. "Full," she said, pointing, pronouncing the word carefully, anxious to be understood.

"Yes," I agreed. "A full moon." I thought of Carl in the darkness of the cave. I thought of going upstairs after dinner to my comfortable little room. I was not going to sleep. I saw myself lying awake hour after hour tossing and turning. I thought of Carl emerging in the morning to find no one had cared enough to be there, waiting to see him safe. I thought of other things. Things I would not allow my mind to dwell on. Things Luigi and the police as well as Andrew had said would not happen if Carl was sensible and stayed where he was.

But it had not been sensible to go into the grotto in the first place. I put my napkin down. Warmed by the wine, refreshed by the meal, I thought with the help of moonlight of this calibre I should be able to easily find a way in to the wasteground from the road above the Villa Passerina and thence to the steps that led down to the water.

I pushed my chair back, lifted my head and became aware of a man, Andrew, standing awkwardly between a pillar and the door leading into the foyer of the hotel. I sat down again with a thump. He came forward. Pulled out the chair opposite and sat down.

I said, "Don't say anything, Andrew."

"Now look, my dear," he sounded sensible and rather distant like a schoolteacher chastising a child, "you can't walk out in a huff like that."

I said distinctly, "You may remember, I was asked to leave. I'm sorry about Carl. And I'm very, very sorry indeed to have disrupted your – your—" I sought for a suitable word to tactfully convey my regret at causing the Villa Passerina to give up black emotions that should never have been disturbed. I had to leave the sentence unfinished. "I shall go home as soon as I've seen Carl safe. Then you must forget me."

"You're being melodramatic," he said tersely.

So much for my certainty that I was being cool.

"You know perfectly well that what's done cannot be undone," he said. "Donna and the children have taken you to their hearts." He offered a conciliatory hand across the table.

I kept mine safely beneath the table cloth. I didn't want to be reinstated because my stepfamily had taken me to their hearts. "The timing was wrong," I said.

"How could it have been otherwise?"

If you hadn't voluntarily opted out of my life it could have been otherwise, I thought, but I had lost the right to blame him. I thought of Carl's story splashed in newsprint across the world. Of Andrew saying, 'Jane did that to me.' Donna riposting, 'Look what you did to her,' and the atmosphere of the Villa Passerina never quite the same again.

"I am going down to the grotto," I said, rising again from my seat. "Signor Vallini has talked to me about it. You may not know, but children have been cut off in that cave before now. It's thought to be safe enough. No one seems to have thought about telling his mother, by the way."

Andrew rose also. "Why should we worry her? She would lose a night's sleep, that's all. As you say, others have been cut off in the past. The police aren't bothered. But why should you go down at this late hour? There's nothing you can do."

"Someone should be there. Besides, I want to. Goodnight," I said. "I'm going up to change." I left him there and ran up the stairs, changed hurriedly into a jumper, jeans and anorak, and ran down again with Carl's jacket over my arm. Andrew was gone but when I came down the hotel steps he was waiting in the little parking place, standing by an impressive-looking BMW that dwarfed Carl's Karmann Ghia. He opened the door as I approached. The moonlight was not so bright here without the white-painted walls, but it was bright enough. I reckoned I could find my way by it down into the bay.

I slid into the passenger seat. It took only a few moments to run down into the town then up the winding road opposite, retracing my long and anguished journey. We didn't talk, but as he pulled up outside the villa Andrew said, "I wish you wouldn't, but if you must I'll come with you."

"There's no need," I said as I slipped out. "Anyway, if the water's still rough I won't stay."

He glanced at the watch on his wrist. "You realise, I suppose, it's after eleven?"

I wasn't concerned about the time. Only that the moon would

stay away from clouds, that the sea would calm and that Andrew would not be on hand with his anger when Carl emerged.

"I really don't like you going—"

I shut off his concern. "I'm very athletic. Very strong. And very sensible," I said, thinking he would have known that if he had been around for the last twenty-six years. I shut the car door carefully and slipped through the gate into his garden.

The path was less slippery now, having been dried by a balmy breeze. The steps, though, were night-black. The moon is not like the sun. It takes the darkness out of the air and off the water, but not the land. These cliff steps tonight were hideously dangerous. I picked my way carefully, taking my time and was relieved to reach the bottom without falling.

The rocks on the shoreline were great threatening monsters in the moonlight. I could hear the water hissing and lapping below and around them. I felt with my feet for safe places in their shadows. I pressed my hands against their solid bulk as I edged round them. I scrambled across the shale and stumbled up the rocky incline onto the grass. Andrew had been right to be concerned for my safety.

The sea on my right was silvery in the moonlight. Calmer? I thought so, though the water was still turbulent near the entrance to the grotto. I went as close as I dared but there was nothing to see. Nothing but darkness. A great black hole in the cliff. I climbed a little way up the bank, found a niche in a rock and sat down with Carl's coat over my knees. I was glad I had come. Pointless my vigil might be, but there was a rightness about it that satisfied me.

The sea sounds lulled my senses. I allowed myself to sink. To dream. After a while I knew I was drifting. I allowed myself to go. Into my dream Evelina Lambardini came. And then that name Frattuni. It seemed intensely significant. Frattuni. I struggled to regain consciousness. I wanted to consider and dissect this new knowledge that Frattuni was important. I had gone down too far. I took the name with me into the muddle of my worried dreams.

I awoke with a start. What had wakened me? The night was silent except for the sea sounds. I rubbed my eyes. Light was coming out of the sky, enfolding the moon, taking its shape and clarity away. I tried to read the time by my watch, blinked, then looked again. Was the hour hand pointing to five? I couldn't be sure.

I climbed stiffly to my feet and stumbled down the steep little slope. I stood looking at the water as it fled into the mouth of the grotto. Fled, that was the word. Last night it had still been hurling itself. Now it seemed merely to flee from the greater ocean as though its last hours of playing wild games in the grotto were coming to a close. As though its power was being taken away. I ventured close to the mouth. Watched it flow in. I had a sense of waiting. Something was going to happen. The something that had wakened me.

The water fled back, merged with its greater self, flowed in again. It was quiet now, and swift, as though a game was being played, the grotto drawing it in, the sea sucking it out. There was a rhythm to its coming and going. In. Out. I stood watching it, mesmerised, knowing that this was the moment. That something would happen because the sea was ready.

And then, without surprise, I saw the canoe. It came like the wind, fast and silent, sweeping past me. I cried out but Carl would not have heard me. He was flying with the stream, out and out. The water lifted high and higher still, changed its mind, flattened out.

I held my breath. Strained my eyes. Waited. My heart stopped beating. The moon had gone. The darkest hour comes before the dawn. I felt myself engulfed in darkness. I shouted. Shouted until I was hoarse. The sea sounds absorbed my cries. Then I thought I saw something rising and falling on the swell.

Chapter Eleven

"Carl!" I shouted, "Carl!" The shape took form, moved nearer. A man in a canoe. I thought that was what I saw because it was what I expected to see. "Carl!"

And then came an answering shout, "Hi! Is anyone there?"

I felt a surge of triumph because it was right that I should have come back. He had expected it. "Jane!" I shouted. "It's Jane!" An early morning breeze feathered past me, taking my cries in to the cliff. The canoe came closer. Slid into the funnel that was feeding the grotto. I held my breath. Then it swung round. I could see now. Carl was paddling frantically. The canoe shot forward, swept across the shore line, then turned and headed in towards the boulders.

"Carl!" I shouted. He heard me.

"Hi!"

I found my way down among the jumble of rocks. Reached out and grasped the nose of the canoe. Pulled it in. He clambered up beside me. Took over. I scrambled back onto the sea grass and stood waiting while he dragged the canoe in.

"Whew!" he said.

I looked up at him. Saw the excitement of the escape was in him still. "You gave us quite a scare," I said, as though there was no more to the passions and emotions of the night than that.

"Oh hell! I'm sorry." He wiped his wet hair back from his forehead. "I didn't judge that very well, after all. I was getting bored." He glanced around, then back to me. "What are you doing here, all alone?"

"I was worried. That you might get bored, as you said."

"Would you have dived in and saved me?" He looked at me closely. His eyes were quizzical.

"Yes," I replied. "Yes, I think so."

"And we'd both have drowned."

"Not necessarily. I'm a good swimmer." I had to remember he was to marry another woman so I said, "I'm not the only person who cared. The police were here. And the family. Especially Guido. He had to go to bed, of course. I couldn't sleep."

"Ah! So you couldn't sleep. There's typical British phlegm for you." He kissed me with his wet mouth. The water from his hair rained down on my face.

I kissed him back with passion, thinking of Evelina and the fact that I might never have another chance.

He released me and stood back. "Sorry, I've made you wet," he said, brushing the water from the front of my anorak.

I smiled at him and felt blessed.

He hauled the canoe up further and leant it against the rugged cliff. "It'll be all right there."

"I've got your coat," I said, picking it up from the rock where I had laid it.

He took it and slung it round his shoulders. "I'm wet through," he said, "and a bit cold. Is your worthy Maria up, do you think? Would she give me breakfast and last night's dinner combined? I could eat a horse."

I gathered up my typical British phlegm and said, "I've news for you. I've been thrown out of the Villa Passerina. You're going to have to walk to your hotel."

"Oh God!" he said. "I'm sorry." He grasped my arm.

I told him about his wallet dropping out of his pocket. "That's it. Let's get going," I said briskly. "We've a hill to climb."

He tightened his grasp on my wrist. "That's not it. Tell me what happened."

I snatched my wrist away. "I don't talk to journalists." Apart from the fact that the circumstances of my going were private, I couldn't trust myself not to break down. I set out in a hurry across the sea grass and the shale behind the boulders, then up on to the cliff path. It was light enough now to see our way. We couldn't talk without stopping and I didn't stop.

We made the top in what must have been record time. The sun was coming up over the mountain. I had always turned right here, heading for the Villa Passerina garden. Now, looking straight ahead, I saw there was a narrow path edging left through the scrub. I followed it and in silence Carl followed me. Fifty yards further on we came to a steep incline that would take us on to the road. I put on speed and hurtled up this last litle rise.

He emerged beside me and took my hand. "Let's run." I took a deep breath and ran with him. There weren't many people around. Those who were making their early morning deliveries looked at Carl oddly. His soaking jeans and shirt clung to his figure. His wet shoes squelched. He was carrying his jacket now.

I thought, as we sped along the front, of the doleful figure I must have presented to onlookers last night, trudging along here with my bag, weighed down more by failure than by my few possessions. I discarded the memory.

We came to the foot of the steps. Carl bounded up. "Hey!" I protested, "I'm not a mountain goat," but I found, after all, I could give a very good imitation of one.

He waited. Took my hand. "It's hunger that's driving me."

"You won't get much here at this hour."

"No. We'll go down to Benjamino's. He'll give us something substantial."

Luigi Vallini, surprisingly, was in the foyer dressed in his neat black suit as though he had not been to bed. He greeted Carl with a raised arm and a shout of congratulatory Italian. A woman in a white apron with a white scarf wrapped round her hair paused, leaned on her mop, listening. Smiling.

Luigi turned to me. "I told you! It is nothing. Here he is! Something to tell his grandchilds, eh? And now you will have breakfast." He gestured towards the tables in the courtyard, dull in the early morning light, the chairs lying upside down on the little tables. It looked very unwelcoming. Carl said we proposed to go down into the town.

"No, no. I will personally see to a special breakfast," Luigi insisted. "What will you have?" He hurled orders at the woman with the mop. She went out of the door that led to the cloisters, heading for the terrace where we had dined that first night. "The sun will be there in a few moments," Luigi declared, optimistically I thought.

Carl said, "Right. Fruit. A five egg omelette." He turned to me. "You will share an omelette?"

"One fifth of it will do very well," I replied, laughing.

He grinned. "You can't imagine how hungry I am."

"I can. Five eggs!"

Luigi went behind the desk and smilingly produced our room keys. "Twenty minutes," he said.

Carl was waiting when I came down after my shower, already halfway through a cup of coffee. The purple flowers on the creeper were opening, smiling on the scene. The sun shone down on the town. I, too, was smiling. Smiling inside because Carl, though he belonged to another woman, was safe.

"Sit down." He jumped up and pulled out a chair for me.

"You're mighty perky for a man who's been up all night," I said.

"What do you mean, up all night? I slept like a log. There's nothing much to do inside a black cave other than sleep, once I'd thought out my article. Don't look so alarmed. A reporter worth his salt will get an article out of every experience."

"This one is on being cut off in a cave?" I asked warily, not entirely trusting him.

"What else? And you? How did you employ your time?"

"Sleeping, also." I felt sheepish, admitting it.

"Lucky I didn't need saving."

"Sorry." And then I remembered that something had come to me in my half awake, half asleep period. A lead as to where I should go. I said, "Evelina sold that picture to Andrew."

If I had dropped a bomb on our breakfast table I couldn't have made more of an impact. Luigi chose that moment to arrive with his tray, filling the air with the scent of hot olive oil and tomatoes, pimentoes and all the delicious scents of an Italian meal. There was a little theatrical drama while with exaggerated flourishes he divided the omelette up between us, a boy brought hot rolls and we made our exclamations of pleasure.

When we were alone again I said, "Sorry if I've put you off your breakfast. I want a favour of you, now. I want you to ask her who Frattuni is. Or rather, where he lives."

"Who is Frattuni?"

"An artist, at a guess. Maybe the one who painted the copy of the Raphael that Andrew is trying to sell."

He dug his fork into the food. "Eat up. It's wonderful."

We didn't talk for a while. I could see his brain ticking over. I could see he needed time. The boy brought some more coffee and took our plates away.

Carl put his elbows on the table and addressed me. "When did she sell him this picture?"

"Eighteen months ago. Why don't you ring her up?"

"Eighteen months ago," he said consideringly, "she was living in Rome."

"She must have come here. Or Andrew might have gone there."

He was silent. It was clear he had a lot to think about. After a while he said, "Can't you ask your father about Frattuni?"

"He doesn't know him. Only the name. Besides, I'm not seeing him again. You ring Evelina," I said.

Carl looked down at the tablecloth, then up at me. I could see he wasn't going to ring Evelina. I was anxious to know why. He said, "Do you think your father is telling the truth?"

I can't imagine why I should have been indignant. I was in disgrace with Andrew. He had thrown me out. The fact that Donna had sent him to apologise and bring me back scarcely counted. I told Carl how I had overheard a conversation between Evelina and Andrew. "She was begging him to withdraw the picture. Yet when I questioned her about it she denied she had even seen Andrew. It was she who lied," I said, allowing my jealousy and my misery to get the better of me.

"When? When did you ask her?"

"In the ladies room when you were waiting at the lift that night the three of us had dinner together. Remember, you asked me what we were talking about."

"So that was what was wrong. I thought there was something."

"What was she doing in Rome?"

He didn't answer immediately. Scarcely realising what I was doing I put a hand over his on the table. I saw his face close. I felt his hand withdraw from beneath mine and thought with despair, I have lost him now. I have lost him because I said Evelina was a liar.

"She did a course at a cookery school in Rome. She was there for about a year, or maybe more. Yes, more I think. "Eighteen months, perhaps." He shook his head.

I could see I had given him a great deal to think about. "What is it?" I asked. "Were you not here?"

"No. I was in England most of the time. But there was a mystery," he admitted. "She wouldn't . . ." His voice trailed away. He frowned at the memory, thinking.

"Wouldn't what?" I asked.

"Oh, I don't know. They couldn't get her to come home for ages. I was going to see her but she put me off." He began to tap his fingers on the table.

"Well," I said sharply, angry in my despair and humiliation, and angry, too, with myself. I was sorry if searching out Frattuni was going to disclose some little indiscretion of Evelina's, but I was going to get to the bottom of this Raphael business. If I couldn't stop Carl writing about my father I was determined he was going to write the truth. I owed Andrew that for bringing Carl to the villa. "Do you know this man Frattuni?"

"No."

"Couldn't you share your thoughts with me?"

"I am thinking that it might not be too difficult to find an artist called Frattuni in Rome," Carl said. "An artist of that calibre, I mean. If Frattuni is an artist."

"Wouldn't it be easier to ask Evelina?"

He did not reply. He stared down at the table, and because his lids were lowered I could not see the expression in his eyes.

There was a sound of footsteps. We both looked up. A youngish man was heading across the paving stones. He came right up to Carl and spoke to him in Italian. Carl waved him away, pushed his chair back, stood up. Luigi came running and protesting, gesticulating. A noisy argument ensued.

"What is it?" I asked when I could get a word in.

Luigi pleaded with me. "It is the press. He must speak to them about being in the grotto. It is good publicity for me."

I threw my head back and roared with delighted laughter. "Hoist with your own petard!" I stood up. "After you've got rid of this frightful nuisance," I said, safe in the knowledge that the reporter did not speak English, "I'll be in my room."

"Damn it," said Carl glaring at me, "this is my story."

"Maybe it's not. Not if he's from a local paper and wants to get the copy in today. You haven't time to write it," I said sweetly.

He glared at me.

"You've got to go to Rome."

He looked wry. "Yes. Get yourself ready. I won't be long."

There was a little pile of brochures on my recessed windowsill. I flicked through them until I found a map of Italy. How many miles from Amalfi to Rome? I looked down at the scale of kilometres. Maybe two hundred and fifty? I glanced across at the telephone. I could ring Evelina myself since Carl was unwilling to do so. But to what purpose? She had already lied to me, denying knowledge of the painting. She could hardly admit to knowledge of the man whom I now suspected of being the artist. And she might put the cat among the pigeons by telling my father. She might even telephone Frattuni and warn him to make himself scarce.

I heard footsteps and Carl appeared in the open doorway. "Right! Are you ready?"

I handed him his wallet and picked up my handbag. "Did you give the reporter a good story?" I asked, looking at him from under my lashes.

"I did indeed." He punched my shoulder gently.

"I'm surprised you gave in. A tough man like you."

"These chaps have to live. Besides, he already had the bones of it from Luigi. I stayed to be sure he got it right."

We started down the steps towards the tiny car park. "What's right and wrong about being cut off in a cave?"

"Just that. As you said it. If you're cut off you're a fool. If you make a considered decision to go in to find out if a canoe is still there with the intention of hauling it up out of reach of the water, knowing the risks—"

"You're a hero," I butted in, finishing for him.

"Something like that. You've got a sharp tongue in your head, Jane Hollis."

We ran down the steps laughing and jumped into the convertible.

Carl frowned at the petrol guage. "I'm going to have to stop for *benzina*."

I felt his use of the Italian word was an indication of the way he was thinking. He wasn't dealing with Andrew in his mind. He was on the trail of something to do with the Italian Evelina. I had the feeling he was taking me, with my concern for Andrew, along for the ride. The green-eyed monster that had me firmly in its grip jolted my senses and I said, "Petrol."

"Yes. Petrol." But he spoke automatically. Then he shook his head as though shaking the Italian intrusion away and said, "You ought to be starting to learn Italian." He started the engine.

"There's no point. I shan't be coming back. By the time you've finished this assignment of yours I'll be thoroughly discredited. I won't dare set foot in Italy again."

The car was creeping down the steep little incline towards the road. "Oh, I don't know," he replied, still absorbed, still far away, "it depends, doesn't it, on what comes out of this?"

"What are you thinking of as the options?"

He didn't answer and I didn't press him. I knew well enough Carl only gave answers when it suited him. I was pretty certain his intention in going to Rome had changed direction. It may have begun with following up his story, but I thought it was now to eliminate Evelina from the scandal.

We whined up the hill then sped down again, along the coast road. The sky was cloudless, the sea still ruffled with white wavelets. He drove fast. My hair streamed out behind me. It was like sitting in the road, we were so low. We swept past high cars and higher buses. The car was like a fast little animal, dashing with its head down and ears back. I didn't feel dwarfed by the larger vehicles, rather that we were a different breed, showing them how they could live if they weren't encumbered with size. I was surprised that Carl liked to drive his mother's Lancia. I wondered now if it was mere politeness and a kindness that he brought me to Amalfi in her car. A promise to return. I certainly could not imagine the dignified Signora Beaumont driving this wild beast.

We wound up the hill on the outskirts of Salerno, passed the grey-roofed houses huddled together as though for protection against the sea, then dived into the green countryside beyond which stretched the autoroute. "Isn't finding an artist in a city a bit like finding a needle in a haystack?" I asked, lifting my voice above the wind.

"The priests are the ones who know everything about everybody."

"What priest? Rome's a big city?"

"I know where to start."

Of course. He knew where Evelina had lived. Had no doubt written to her. Visited her even, prior to the time when she had put him off. Catholics, unlike so many of us Protestants, went to church. It could be easy to trace a priest who knew her, as well as knowing artists in the area.

"Are you going to be hungry?"

"Never again, I should think." I had been given more than one fifth of that great omelette. "We could stop somewhere for a coffee."

"Yes. Let's do that."

We lapsed into silence again. I sensed Carl's head was full of affairs that had nothing to do with me. Matters he wanted to concentrate on. We were coming into Naples. Straight roads, then twists and turns, the railway, suburbia, slums, a long run down a wide avenue, then a side street and a restaurant with vine and decorative lanterns over the door. He parked in that untidy way Italians park their cars, half on the pavement among a jumble of its fellows. Got out. Stretched, then sat down at a pavement table and gave our order. "Five minutes," said Carl looking at his watch.

"How did that watch fare in the water?"

"It's waterproof."

Our coffee came. It wasn't hot. It never is. We drank it swiftly, climbed back into the car and set out again. It was the middle of the afternoon when we came to the outskirts of Rome. Carl drove straight to the centre. We hadn't talked much. I sensed he didn't want to. Between the rooftops I glimpsed the dome of a church. He parked outside.

"Come in if you like," he said. "If you want to see the church."

I said I would and climbed out. We went up the steps. It was quite a small church as Catholic churches go, and less ornate than many I had seen. A young priest was standing near the door. Carl went up to him and spoke to him in Italian. I heard a name. Dominic. So he hadn't been taking pot luck!

He knew the church, and specifically he knew a priest, or at least his name.

The man briskly crossed the aisle and disappeared through a side door, the skirts of his soutane swinging. Carl stood with hands in his trousers pockets looking round as one does in a church, but without interest, as though his mind was on something else. "You've been here before?" I ventured.

He nodded.

It was clear he didn't want to discuss it. I wandered off and examined a few statues. Marvelled at the beautiful marble figures on sarçophagi. Looked up at the stained glass windows, red, blue, green, a wonderful richness of colour glowing in the afternoon sun. Out of the corner of my eye I could see Carl standing feet apart now, pulling at one ear lobe, apparently deep in thought. I wandered on into a little chapel and out again.

Footsteps. A smiling middle-aged priest was hurrying down the aisle, holding out his hand to Carl. A burst of chatter. Much gesticulating. They talked fast. The priest stopped to think, rubbing his forehead. Came up with an answer. Carl took a notebook out of his pocket, tore out a page and handed it to the priest along with a pen. I came slowly back to them hoping the man spoke English so I could hear what he had to say first-hand. The priest handed the paper back then looked curiously at me. I smiled as I came closer and he smiled back, looking at my clothes, my hair as one does when pinpointing a nationality. "You are English, Signorina?"

Carl put the paper back in the notebook back and introduced us. Father Dominic. Jane Hollis.

"You are on holiday, Miss Hollis?"

"Yes. Visiting my father."

"And helping to trace this artist?" Without waiting for a reply he turned back to Carl. "That is the best I can do. I wish you luck. And tell me, how is Evelina?"

"Fine."

"They are living, where? I have not seen them for some time."

Carl frowned. "She is with her parents in Amalfi. We had dinner together recently."

A puzzled look came over Father Dominic's face. He stared

at Carl as though searching for something in his face. Then he addressed him specifically, speaking slowly, seeming to choose his words with care. "She is happy, now?"

Carl laughed. "Why not? Yes, I think she's happy."

The man looked nonplussed. Then he said, "I would like to hear from her. You will convey that message? That I would like to hear from her?"

"Sure." Carl said to me, "We had better be on our way. Thank you very much, Father Dominic."

"You will let me know?"

"About the picture? Yes." Carl looked surprised. "Yes, if you're interested."

"Not about the picture, though I am interested and I wish you luck. I mean, you will . . ." He broke off. "I am concerned for Evelina. If she doesn't get in touch, perhaps you would . . ." He broke off again, searching Carl's face.

He smiled. "She's perfectly all right, I assure you, Father."

Father Dominic didn't reply immediately. He began to turn away. Turned back. "Good," he said. "But let me know, if she does not."

As we came back down the steps I stole a look at Carl's face. He was clearly perplexed, and equally clearly was not going to discuss the matter with me. I climbed into my seat. He opened the notebook and looked down at the paper on which the priest had drawn a little diagram. Then he took a road map out of the glove box. I watched the bustling passers-by, the little cars creeping around looking for parking spaces, the young drivers loudly insulting each other, blasting their horns. A normal Italian scene. Carl folded his map and put it back.

"Well!" he said addressing me at last, looking pleased. "That was a success, in the end."

"He knows Frattuni?"

"No. He gave me the address of a chap called Carboni. He's an artist. Apparently he knows all the rogues in the local art world. And the dealers. And the forgers." Carl was putting the key in the ignition as he spoke, automatically turning the key while still looking down at the paper. "He knows everybody, in fact. He's done a spell in jail for forgery but he's going straight now. Whether he's willing to talk is another matter.

We can but try." Carl shoved the paper into my hands. "Hang on to that."

It was a rough little sketch of a street map with a house marked by a black cross. He started the engine, put the car into gear and swept out of the square, into the rushing traffic once more. "His apartment is on the other side of the river. We have to get across that first."

We threaded our way through the city in surprisingly quick time, dicing dangerously, it seemed to me, with the hordes of little cars, the mopeds and the scooters. We crossed the Tiber and sped into a long, busy thoroughfare. I had my finger on the map. "Turn right here, I think."

He swung the car round. It was a narrow, congested street. The buildings were jumbled together in higgledy-piggledy fashion. Lines of washing were strung across from window to window in the continental way. Carl drove slowly along the street, looking puzzled. "There's not enough light here for an artist," he muttered.

I said that according to the map we had to go right to the end. He put on speed. We came up a rise and there was a very tall, narrow building standing a little apart with a patch of grass beside it and a very tall cypress looking rather dusty and sad. "I believe that's it," I said. "And it has masses of windows to let in light."

"And here's a place to park," said Carl with satisfaction, running up over the kerb.

I laughed, for the first time since the journalist had captured Carl and taken his story. "It seems to me that anywhere in Rome is a place to park." There were cars running up on pavements so pedestrians could barely pass; they were jammed together at the kerb; precariously abandoned at street corners; they nudged up against statues. "You cope very well," I said. "Your Italian side is in the ascendant." He would be in serious trouble if he forgot to change back into the English mode of parking when he got home.

"I'm a bit of a chameleon," he said as he jumped out, holding the door carefully so as not to scratch a smart little Fiat that was now a little too close. "And very handy it is. Do you want to come with me?"

"I'd love to." I certainly did not want to sit alone in that car, waiting for a traffic policeman to come along, angry in a language I did not understand. I recognised that the citizens expected to get away with their awful parking but just in case they were counting on luck I preferred to make myself scarce. I stepped out and we walked up the street together.

The tall building was an apartment block. We went into a narrow, flagged passageway. There was a board on which was printed a list of names. Carl ran his finger down them. "Number fifteen is our man." He glanced round. "I bet there's no lift and he's at the top. Never mind, we've been a long time sitting. And you're in good fettle after your adventures."

We climbed a flight of narrow, dark stairs side by side. The man Carboni did indeed live at the top of the building. We stood on the landing looking round. There was a blue door painted in crazy shapes and lively colours. That had to be it. I pushed the bell. From inside there came a curt shout.

"He wants us to go in." Carl pushed the door wide.

We entered the most untidy and possibly the dirtiest room I have ever been into. There were easels holding half finished canvases, more canvases stacked against walls, tables littered with papers and pots of paint, brushes everywhere. The man himself was dressed in a dirty overall spattered with paint. He was a strange looking fellow, gaunt, with a good deal of dark hair and several teeth missing. His eyes were small and over-bright. His face was pasty. He looked underfed, and worried. I thought he looked like a criminal. But then I am not an expert on Italian criminals.

Carl greeted him. He merely nodded, eyeing me suspiciously, then turned back to Carl. He did not offer us a seat, and indeed I could not see where we might have settled with any degree of comfort. While Carl talked to him I looked round the room. There were a great many paintings here, some traditional, some modern. The man was obviously a very good artist. There was an argument going on. Carboni was waving his arms dismissively. Carl held his ground. Then he felt in his inside jacket pocket and brought out his wallet. Carboni looked consideringly at the notes. Carl added another. Then another. Carboni nodded his head.

The discussion went more easily after that. I wished very much that I spoke Italian. I was dying to know what was being said.

After a while Carboni took a pencil from a drawer, found a piece of paper, wrote something down and handed it to Carl. Another discussion ensued with more arm waving, though of a passive type. He seemed to be giving directions.

"*Ciao,*" Carl said heading towards the door.

"*Ciao,*" I ventured tentatively. He grunted.

"What luck?" I asked as we began to descend the stairs.

"A good deal." He looked pleased. He took the stairs with a swing in his step. "Let's hop in the car and get moving. We've a fair way to go."

"Does he know Frattuni?"

"Yes."

Chapter Twelve

We sped down the three flights and ran back to the car. Carl told me, as we hurried through the busy streets and headed out of town, what Carboni had to say.

"The picture, this Raphael or so-called Raphael, was brought to Carboni by Seizerk, the American art dealer who sold the allegedly original Raphael to the Bolivian millionaire."

"Where did he get it?"

"From this chap Frattuni. Cesario Frattuni. We're going to look for him now. At the time he lived in Rome but his family owns a farm about seventy kilometres southwest of here and that's where it seems we'll find him."

"Why did the American take the picture to Carboni?"

"He wanted a copy. Apparently Carboni is a pretty good forger, or was, until he did that spell in jail."

"Did he tell you?"

"No. The priest said so. Anyway, he's going straight and doesn't take chances these days. He reckons the picture that was brought to him—"

"*Madonna and Child*?"

"Yes. He reckons it was an original. He says he'd stake his life on it. But Seizerk told him it was merely a good copy. Seizerk was very laid back about it. He said he was trying to buy it from Frattuni but Frattuni wouldn't sell so he had decided he wanted a copy to take back for himself."

"With the owner's permission?"

"So Seizerk said."

"Not everyone has his price, then?"

"Apparently there was some sentimental value attached to this picture. And I suppose Frattuni didn't need the money. He may be rich. Who knows? We may be about to find out." Carl reached into the glove box, produced a map and tossed it into my lap. "See if you can find a road leading off to Alatri. That's the area we want."

I searched while he kept his eyes on the road. "Here it is." I marked it with my forefinger. "If you see a sign for Frisonone you've gone too far. That's the best I can do for the moment. Keep driving. Map reading is not one of my talents."

We were out on the open road now. Carl put his foot down. The sun was sinking in the west. Even in summer – it might be autumn to the Italians, already in their wool suits but it was still summer to me – the darkness came early.

"Go on with the story. So the art dealer brought it to Carboni and asked him to do a copy."

"Carboni says he wasn't interested but Seizerk's fee went up and up until he couldn't refuse. It was then he started to smell a rat. Seizerk swore he didn't intend to sell the copy but Carboni was nervous. So he put his mark on the copy."

"What's that?" I had forgotten about looking for road signs. I was already one jump ahead. What was in my father's copy of the *Madonna and Child* that was not in the original? When we knew that we would be well along the road to the truth.

"A bird," said Carl.

"A what?"

"Yes, a bird. Carboni painted it in at the top right-hand corner beside a cloud effect. He said it's almost undetectable, but it's there, and it's his defence if things go wrong."

"Presumably he didn't tell the American?"

"No. So it's possible that this indignant Bolivian millionaire has a *Madonna and Child* with a tiny bird, maybe only visible under a magnifying glass, tucked away in the background."

"Unless he didn't take the original back," I put in. "Unless he swapped them." Carl raised one eyebrow. "So we're not going to see the picture," I said. "Evelina sold it to Andrew who sent it to Amsterdam. Why are we going to see this chap Frattuni? Ought we not to be going to Amsterdam? Or even back to the Villa Passerina to see if Andrew spotted a bird when he did the copy?"

Carl didn't answer and I knew. Had known since I had first told him about Evelina's part in this mystery. He wanted to see Frattuni and that was about the mystery of why Evelina hadn't come home from Rome for over a year. The picture was only incidental.

We didn't miss the side road. "You're too modest about your talents," Carl said as he swung the little car round and we headed in towards the hills. On either side of the road lay ochre coloured farmhouses with their ancient outbuildings and stacks of logs ready for the winter. He allowed the car to slow down, took out of his pocket the sheet of paper Carboni had given him and spread it against the steering wheel. "No use giving you this," he said. "It's in Italian. He's omitted to tell us how far up the road we go." He turned the paper round, squinted at a bit of scribble and added, "Ah, yes. It's the big one. The biggest."

We were approaching a rise. The road wound up for a couple of hundred yards and there on our left was a house, not very different from those we had seen except that this one was bigger than the others and had an air of past grandeur. It lay at the top of the rise, squat and square with wings spread out on either side. The roof was made of dark red tiles like split drainpipes. Tall green cypresses stood stiffly sentinel in a row behind it, their upright bearing in sharp contrast to the soft warm stone. The farm buildings too were old and had fallen into partial decay.

"It doesn't look the sort of house to be harbouring a valuable picture," I ventured, considering its dilapidation. Carl also looked uncertain. He drove past. There were some more dwellings further on but they were small and less likely still. He turned the car in a gateway and we went back.

"This has to be it," he said.

I climbed out and opened the gate. The drive that might once have been gravelled had through neglect become more of a farm track. I shut the gate and walked behind the car. Carl drove up the side of the house. We were looking into a tidy yard. There was no one in sight. A tan and white mongrel with a dusty, untidy coat lay on its side on a flagstoned area in the sun. It rose to its feet and uttered a half-hearted bark. On the right was a netted enclosure with a structure at the end, half shed, half box, from which came the scuffle and cheep of chickens.

"We had better go to the front door," Carl said.

We went along an overgrown path past some tall bushes. There were vines everywhere, climbing up the walls, trailing over neglected trellises in the garden. Several of the painted green shutters on the upper floor were closed. The rays of the setting sun glinted on large windows on either side of the heavy front door.

There was an enormous bell with a rope trailing down from the wall. Carl pulled it. The peal might have wakened the dead. We stood back in alarm. There were voices from within. The cry of a small child. The door opened and a good-looking man wearing untidy overalls opened the door.

"*Buon giorno.*"

"*Buon giorno,*" we said and Carl asked, "Signor Frattuni?"

He nodded. "*Si.*" He was an extraordinarily attractive man. Heavy, muscular, darkly handsome. Carl spoke to him at length in Italian. He looked surprised, and certainly interested. He gestured that we should come in. As I stepped over the doorstep he looked at me hard. "You are English, Signorina?"

"Yes." Nobody ever took me for an Italian.

"My mother will be pleased." He spoke virtually without an accent. "She doesn't have anyone to speak with here." He walked ahead, leading us into a big sitting room, low ceilinged and full of the heavy, dark Italian furniture that looks as though it will last forever regardless of treatment. He motioned to us to sit down, then went through an inside door calling, "*Mama.*"

I looked round. The drapes were made of good material but they were old and faded. The carpet, by contrast, was new and very beautiful. There were two glass fronted cabinets containing some exquisite ornaments, good china, and on the walls several very grand-looking gilt framed mirrors that looked rather out of place in the setting. The only pictures were a couple of pleasant prints, one depicting a mountain scene with blood-red poppies in the foreground, the other a seascape.

His mother was about forty-five or fifty, a tired-looking woman. Rather beautiful. She came in carrying a child. She had a singularly aristocratic air which her son had not. Her hair was a little untidy. She brushed it back with one hand. The child was a beauty. Perhaps a year old, or a little less. It had the man's large dark eyes and a shock of blonde curls. Boy or girl? I couldn't tell. Frattuni spoke to his mother in Italian. She too looked surprised, then pleased.

"Good afternoon," she said and smiling at me said, "Now that I am living here I do not often have an opportunity to talk English. Until eighteen months ago I lived in Rome where I had many English friends. I speak it now to the child and to my son, but it is not like talking to an English person. Won't you sit down?"

I chose an enormous, ornately carved armchair standing beside an open fireplace. The fire box was artistically arranged with logs and wild flowers. Carl sat down on a stiff wooden sofa.

"So, you have come about the picture," she said.

Carl reached into his inside pocket, brought out a card and handed it to her. She glanced round as though looking for something then held it up to the light to read. I saw a pair of glasses on a small table, jumped up and handed them to her.

She smiled. "I can just about read it. Ah!" She handed the card back, nodding. "A reporter. So, how did you find us?"

"I believe you know a friend of mine," said Carl. "Evelina Lambardini."

Her glance went directly to the child. "She was to have been my daughter-in-law," the woman said, then added bitterly, "But now we have lost our money—"

Her son broke in. "*Mama*!" he said sharply, silencing her. She backed on to a sofa and sat down. He said to us, "This was my grandfather's farm where we came for holidays. Things have gone wrong for us. My father died leaving many debts. I have lost my business. Now my mother must care for the child. And I live here and work the farm which became run down after my grandfather died. Anyway," he said, glancing across at the baby, "it is better for my daughter." He smiled. The baby waved an arm at him, crowing.

I did not dare look at Carl. I had an impression, seeing only out of the corner of my eye, that his face was very still. Was this Evelina's child? Had we, in coming here, solved the mystery Carl mentioned of why she wouldn't come home? I remembered the priest asking, not after Evelina but after 'them', then going quiet when we did not react.

"So what about the picture?" asked Signora Frattuni. "It has been offered for sale and they are saying it is a forgery."

"That it may be a forgery," Carl corrected her. "Can you tell me something about its history?"

I was thinking that one segment of the history of the picture was that it had been given to Evelina to sell around eighteen months ago, which was when the family came here because they had lost their money. When she would have been a couple of months pregnant. Presumably she came here to have the child.

Frattuni seated himself beside Carl on the sofa.

"What is your interest?"

Carl said, "I'm researching the story behind the picture. It seems there may be several copies." He told them how we had been to see the artist Carboni.

"Ah!" the mother broke in, eyes suddenly alight. "So that is the name of the man who did the copy! We never knew." She repeated bitterly, "Of course we never knew."

"You don't object to publicity?" Carl asked.

Mother and son exchanged glances. He lifted his shoulders, then dropped them. "We have nothing to lose," he said. He turned to Carl, "You would pay us? You must understand we have fallen on hard times."

"Of course," Carl said.

Frattuni rose and went to stand by the mantelpiece, leaning against it. "I have to start at the beginning. In the war. At the end of the war when the Allies were advancing across Europe and the defeated armies had scattered. My grandfather was one of those who lost his regiment. He was a foot soldier. He was making his way home as best he could. You know there was a great deal of looting from the big houses?"

Carl nodded. "So I understand."

"Many of the troops took what they could. Those who had jeeps were able to help themselves to some valuable works of art. A soldier who was sheltering in a big house, an American called Seizerk—"

Carl blinked. "Seizerk? That's—"

Frattuni said, "Yes, this American art dealer who is in all the papers making a fuss about the picture is the grandson of that man who looted the picture in 1945. He knew the story, you see. He came to Europe armed with this address and came to see my grandfather. It was not long before my grandfather died."

Carl said, "Could we go back to the looting. Do you know the name of the people, or the house, it came from?"

"No. I don't think my grandfather was too bothered about anything more than getting home. It was a bad time. It was just a big house, he said. The kind of house one would expect to find valuables in.

"There was a soldier there selling off the pictures from this house to the troops passing through. He offered this one to my grandfather for a very small sum. My grandfather said no. Then, when he was back in the jeep, he changed his mind and asked the driver to wait. He wasn't concerned that the picture might be valuable. He had nothing to take home for the family. He thought at least here was a present. The boys in the jeep agreed to wait and he went back into the house. While he was inside the Allies came over dropping bombs. They missed the house. The men in the jeep must have thought the plane intended to attack the house. They made off down the road and got a direct hit. They were blown to bits."

"So your father's life was, literally, saved by the picture?"

"Yes. And his companions were killed. I have heard him say that picture symbolised so much of what had happened. He treasured it. He kept it on the wall here." Our eyes followed his pointing finger. There was a patch on the wallpaper darker than the rest.

"Then one day, shortly before my grandfather died, as I said, this American turned up and introduced himself as the grandson of the soldier from whom my grandfather had bought the picture. His name was Seizerk."

Carl started. "This is the man—"

"Yes. The one who insists he sold a genuine Raphael to a Bolivian millionaire. He said his American grandfather was curious to know what had happened to the picture. This is fifty years later, you understand. The grandson wanted to buy it and take it back to him."

"Did he say it was valuable, at the time?"

"No." Frattuni gave us a dry little smile. "No. Of course not. He had a good look at it. I was here at the time. 'Sentimental value only,' he said. We believed him. We're not into art. He is. The signature, if there had been one, had disappeared. I dare say it badly needed a clean."

"Your grandfather didn't sell?"

"My father-in-law would not sell," said Signora Frattuni. "For him it had great sentimental value. And besides, he wasn't interested in money. He never had been. He was a simple man. Not educated in the arts. Not very well educated at all. He was very attached to the land. And to his family. He worked hard to see that his children acquired a good education. My husband was a lawyer—" She caught her son's eye and broke off. "I'm sorry. Yes. You must go on with the story." The baby leaned its head against her shoulder. Its eyelids drifted down.

"No," the son went on. "He wouldn't let it go. He said it had brought him luck and he was going to hang on to it for the duration of his lifetime. None of the family needed money at the time. He later gave me permission to sell it after his death. He didn't expect us to feel the same way about it as he did.

"Seizerk pointed out the two men were the same age. That if I were to sell it after my grandfather's death there was a fair chance Seizerk senior would also have expired. In the end, being an old softie as you might say, my grandfather allowed him to take it to Rome to have a copy made. My grandfather trusted people. He was of the old school. Seizerk produced credentials. And you understand he had been very insistent that the painting was of little value. My grandfather expected people to tell the truth. He was not a man of the world."

Our hostess allowed herself a scornful exclamation. "Yes, he had a kind heart, but that didn't mean he was a fool."

Her son continued, "Seizerk didn't bring the painting back. He sent someone else. When my grandfather said he had expected Seizerk to come himself and bring the copy to show him, this man said he couldn't discuss the matter. He hadn't even seen the picture. He didn't know the name of the artist who had done the copy. He said he had to get away. He had a plane to catch. But my grandfather made him wait while he unpacked the picture."

"He was suspicious?"

"Oh yes. His suspicions were aroused. He refused to take delivery."

"So, did Seizerk come?" I asked.

Signora Frattuni laughed. "This is the funny part. My father-in-law, as I said, was not sophisticated, but he knew how to look after things."

"That was when the trouble started," her son said, also smiling. "The man kept insisting he had a plane to catch. He was flying to Los Angeles that evening. So he couldn't take the picture with him. He said Seizerk was waiting for him at the airport. 'In that case,' my grandfather said, 'I'll get the police to pick him up.'" Frattuni and his mother laughed at the memory. I had the impression it was an often-told family joke. "Then my grandfather, who was a man of many parts, slipped out and demobilised his car."

We were all laughing now.

The Signora shook her head ruefully. "He would have looked very silly indeed if he had not had right on his side."

"Did the the police come?" I asked.

"No. He suddenly decided Seizerk might not after all have left his hotel."

The Signora was enjoying herself now. "Cesario," she said, expansively, "you must offer our guests an aperitif." The strain in her face had fallen away.

Carl looked at me. "You're the one who's driving," I said.

"Why not?" he agreed. "*Grazie*."

"Thank you," I added, reminding them that I didn't speak Italian. I didn't want to miss any of the story.

Cesario went to a cupboard and brought out a bottle of vermouth. "I cannot help, you understand," said his mother. "The child is asleep." She looked up at her son. "I will go on a bit?"

He nodded and reached up for some glasses.

"In the meantime, I telephoned the only art critic I knew and begged him to rush out. Ah!" she said with satisfaction. "What it is to have good friends."

"This Seizerk, he was bold as brass. Deeply insulted by my grandfather's suspicions. Full of goodwill." Cesario paused in the act of filling a glass. "He came laden down with Chianti, do you remember, Mama?"

"I do." She was reliving the experience with a touch of glee.

"And of course he had good reason to be confident," said the son as he handed the glasses out. "My grandfather couldn't see the difference between the two pictures. The artist – Carboni, you say the name was?"

Carl nodded.

"He made a wonderful copy. Grandfather admitted he would have been taken in but for Mama's friend, who arrived within fifteen minutes and, what is that good English phrase – put the cat among the pigeons?"

"I can imagine," I said, laughing because English colloquialisms always sound a little absurd coming off a foreign tongue. We sipped our drinks.

"This friend of mine, he had brought a magnifying glass," the signora continued. "He immediately attributed the picture to Raphael. That was the first we knew, but whether one of them was an original or not he couldn't say. He examined them very closely."

"Did Seizerk look nervous?"

"Not noticeably," Cesario replied. "My mother's friend located a small distortion in the cloud effect up in the top right-hand corner. Like a tiny pair of wings. When he showed it to my grandfather, my grandfather said it hadn't been there before. After all, he'd been admiring it for fifty years. He knew the detail."

"A bird?" I asked. "Could it have been a tiny bird?"

Frattuni looked surprised. "It could have been. Yes. Why do you ask?"

I left Carl to tell him. He was the one who had talked to Carboni. The baby yawned and opened her eyes. I rose from my chair, put the glass down and crossed the room. I could see now that this could easily be Evelina's child. It had the same eyes. The same pale gold hair. I didn't think Evelina's was natural any more, but it had probably been like this originally.

The mother spoke to me. "Do you know Evelina sold this picture for a million and a quarter lire?"

I nodded.

"She sold it to a man who has a reputation for fraud."

"She sold it to my father." I recognised immediately the words were out that I should not have embarrassed her like that. Carl glanced at me. His face was quite expressionless. I looked down at my shoes. I didn't know what had prompted me to make that unconsidered remark but I did know that I was emotionally disturbed by seeing Carl in shock from the discovery that the girl he was going to marry had a child by another man. I wondered if he was thinking with the Italian half of his brain, facing up to the fact that the girl he loved was capable of abandoning her child.

"I am sorry," the signora was saying with great dignity. "I would not have said that had I known. Perhaps you would like another aperitif?" She rose and put the baby down on the floor. It crawled a little way then stopped to examine a pattern in the carpet.

"Thank you," I said. After all, I wasn't driving. And it might dull my nerves. I turned to Cesario. "So, how was the situation resolved?"

"My grandfather showed them the door. He was very angry indeed."

"Did he not wonder, then," I asked, "if the painting was valuable? A genuine Raphael? Since Seizerk had gone to so much trouble to get it."

"He was old. He loved his picture. Nobody in the family needed the money at the time." He hesitated. "I know only what I have read in the papers. It is thought that this picture is a genuine Raphael. You may know your father did not give Evelina the price of a Raphael." He looked at me thoughtfully.

"I understand that at the time he believed it to be a copy." I repeated the story Andrew had told me about going to Florence and spending time examining a genuine Raphael *Madonna*. "It was after that he began to wonder if it was genuine."

"Evelina sold it to him because we needed the money. It was for the child."

I thought of the Lambardini parents and Carl's mother who, not knowing they had a granddaughter, were intent upon Evelina marrying Carl. I saw why she was so anxious for Andrew to withdraw the Raphael. She could be thinking of Frattuni as waiting with the child to come forward to claim his share. Frattuni with his offer of marriage and his patience. I wondered if she was living in a state of panic, pretending to herself this episode in her life hadn't happened; if, given time, and reunited with the child, she might come to her senses. She had been in love with this man before.

And then I remembered, she couldn't count on Andrew giving her a share of the money. Exposure was what she was afraid of, with no happy ending. I did not see Evelina as the wife of a poor Italian farmer of peasant stock. But back in Rome as a businessman with money to spend on her he could be a very attractive option.

I said boldly, "I really have no right to speak for my father, but—" I broke off, thinking of Donna, who loved everybody. It was possible she loved Evelina. And certainly she would be touched by the story. Not only that but she would be appalled that Evelina had left her baby for any reason at all. She might even be doubly shocked at hearing the reason, that the lifestyle of the father did not suit her. The signora did not like living here in the country, cut off from her friends. How much more passionately would Evelina feel, she who was young and beautiful? I was suddenly aware that they were all looking at me expectantly, waiting for me to finish the sentence I knew I had no right to formulate.

Carl said, "There is an English saying. If I read Jane's expression correctly, she thinks her father would 'see you right'. If the picture is genuine it will fetch more than either family could possibly need."

"*If* it is genuine." The signora looked out of the window and into the distance. Her shoulders slumped as though she was dispirited by the view of dry baked land rolling away into the distance. She said, or rather murmured, "I would like to get out of here. Back to Rome."

Cesario said, and I thought I detected just a hint of criticism in his voice, "We are very lucky to have had the farm to come to. My mother has been an angel. She sold her home to help pay the debts. But she is past the age where she wants to be tied to such a small child."

"The mother would not marry him," Signora Frattuni said bitterly.

Cesario looked down. The child gazed up at him. His eyes were soft. "In Italy it is the law that the father is responsible. He has custody of the child. The mother cannot take it away. I think she might come back and marry me if we got out of here. She sends what money she can. She is not unfeeling."

I could not look at Carl. I stared at the floor, thinking of the old car Evelina drove which did not accord with her apparent lifestyle and her clothes. I remembered thinking there had to be a reason.

When we left at last, dusk was falling and the ancient, ragged farm buildings were taking on mysterious, muted shapes in the gloom. We went down the overgrown path beneath the darkened trees and round to the side of the farmhouse where we had parked the car. The dog had gone, the chickens were quiet, ready for night. Carl did not speak. I began to feel cold. I climbed into the car. He started the engine and backed out into the road, still without speaking. That's life, I said to myself. That's what happens when you go around looking under stones.

As we sped down the road I could think only of Evelina. Was she in love with Carl, or merely desperate to get out of her situation? To live in a foreign country where she would not be tempted to see her child and the exceptionally attractive man she chose not to live with because he could not give her the lifestyle to which she was accustomed?

Carl said, "We'll soon be on the autoroute." I felt he was a thousand miles from me. "You can sleep."

"Yes." I took it as an order. He wanted to be alone. I closed my eyes. It had been a long day. I was physically and emotionally exhausted. Was it only last night that Carl had been shut in the cave and I wakeful on my vigil among the rocks outside? It might have been a hundred years away. Night was falling blackly around us. The noise of the car engine was soothing. I drifted, dreaming muddled dreams of wild waves, my father's anger, Carl disappearing into the distance, calling, and myself in a state of despair. I wakened with a start and sat up, still half drugged with sleep.

"Where are we?"

"In the car park at the Maria Convento. Do you want to stay here, or go to the villa?"

"What time is it?"

"Nearly nine."

I shook myself awake. I said, "I can't go to the villa." I wondered why he was giving me the option.

"You're going to have to look at that picture," he said, and waited.

I couldn't think. My brain simply wouldn't work. I was aware of being very hungry. I said, "It will have to wait until morning. Do you realise we haven't eaten since breakfast?"

"Yes," he said. "So, I'll drop you here. You'll be able to get some dinner."

I waited for him to tell me where he was going, for clearly he was going somewhere. He hadn't turned the engine off.

"Okay," he said. "I'll see you in the morning."

"*Ciao*," I muttered as I climbed out. I can't think why. I wasn't entirely certain of the meaning of the word. I hoped it meant 'see you soon'. My tired brain was not at that moment into dissecting human reactions. I thought as I climbed the steps and the little car sped off that it was just as well we shouldn't have dinner together. There was too much we couldn't discuss. I wondered if he had decided to have this Frattuni business and the problem of the baby out with Evelina right away. It seemed unlikely. Was he going to talk to his mother? I felt the answer to that was a very definite no. Carl was a man who made his own decisions.

Luigi Vallini met me in the foyer, all smiles. "You have had a nice day?"

"Fascinating," I replied.

"You will have dinner?" He gestured towards the little courtyard from which came laughter and the scatter of Italian voices. I peered round the corner. "It seems to be full."

"No, no. There will be a table for you. Signor Beaumont is not with you?"

"He had to dine elsewhere," I said. I headed for the stairs. "I'll go and change."

It was an extraordinary anti-climax to the day. I dutifully changed into my yellow skirt and top then went back downstairs. Luigi led me to a little table right in a corner. I felt abandoned. Lonely. He must have realised something was wrong for he came several times and stood by my table making pleasantries.

"Signor Beaumont has recovered from his adventure?"

"Oh yes. I think he enjoyed it."

"The chicken is very good tonight. An exceptional herb sauce our chef has made."

I said I would have that. I was not interested in food tonight, only in filling my stomach, which was beginning to rumble and groan. Luigi went away and came back with a bottle of wine. "No, thank you."

"It is on the house, as you say." He gave me his expansive smile.

"Thank you. You know I am not accustomed to having wine every night."

"It is good for you. Will help you to sleep."

Perhaps it would. Perhaps if I drank enough I might not lie awake wondering what a man would do when he found the girl he loved had a child by someone who was still in love with her. With whom she might be still in love. I lifted the bottle and filled my glass to the brim.

I wakened from a dreamless sleep to another of those cloudless Italian days. I stretched luxuriously, feeling grateful for the deep sleep. And then I remembered. I shot out of bed, showered and dressed, all the while trying not to think about Carl, who had disappeared. And why. As I was brushing my hair in front of the mirror it came to me what I must do and I didn't need Carl to help me. I had to go back to the Villa Passerina and see that picture Andrew had painted for the nuns at Guido's school. But how could I? *Easily*, this well rested early morning persona said to me. *Tell Andrew the story*. I hesitated, brush in hand. Would it hold up without mention of Evelina? If I said merely that Frattuni was a friend of hers? *Yes*.

As I ran downstairs I was wondering what kind of Italian shop would sell a magnifying glass. No doubt Luigi would be able to tell me. He was there in the foyer, as usual, with the hotel reins firmly in his hands. "You are ready for breakfast? Signor Beaumont is out there." He gestured towards the vine hung terrace that caught the early morning sun. He saw my expression and wandered off wearing a secret smile.

I was dumbfounded, but only for a moment or two. I hurried outside. Carl was sitting at one of the little tables making short work of a couple of fried eggs. He looked up with a welcoming smile. *"Buon giorno."*

"*Buon giorno*," I replied and before he could jump up pulled out a chair for myself.

"Yes. You're getting quite fluent, aren't you? *Ciao* last night. And now this."

The waiter came and I ordered coffee and a boiled egg. "I don't see why I should eat those dreary rolls. They can make an exception of me, too." I was lighthearted. I was so happy to see him, and in such good humour.

"Providing the establishment can knock up an egg cup."

"I'll hold it in my napkin if they can't." I smiled at him. "And where did you get to last night?"

"Benjamino's," he said. "I had to be by myself for a while to think."

I was flabbergasted and evidently looked it for he said, "Sorry to dump you like that. I couldn't very well explain. I hoped you would understand. This assignment has proved more complicated than I anticipated."

Yes, I thought, he hadn't expected Evelina to be involved. "And what have you decided?" I managed when my breath returned.

"That you and I will go and see your father bearing a magnifying glass."

"I had already made that decision," I told him, "though you weren't in my plans."

"I am now," he said in that endearing style of his and swallowed the last mouthful of egg.

"He's not going to show you that picture. He didn't even show it to me. You're the enemy, remember," I said.

"We'll play it by ear, shall we?"

"Such confidence!"

"You'd never get anywhere without it."

I was nervous of his reception. "I expect he'll throw you out," I said.

"I've been thrown out of better places than the Villa Passerina. You get used to it in my job."

We walked through the town, and slowly up the hill on the winding road below which lay the Villa Passerina. We hadn't had to buy a magnifying glass. Luigi was able to provide one. The gate was not locked. I opened it and we went down the steps. Maria greeted us with a great cry of joy. She wore her feelings fully exposed. Donna came running and flung her arms round me, then, "Hello, Carl," she said warmly holding out a hand.

"Signora."

"Oh, Jane, I am so very pleased you came back. You have brought your bag?" She looked round with a touching mixture of hope and excitement.

"Not yet," I said.

"But you will. You must. Now I'll go and get Andrew. He's in his studio. He has been worrying about you." She led the way out onto the terrace. "I cannot describe to you Guido's face when he rushed in to say his canoe was safe," she said, addressing Carl directly. "That was wonderfully kind of you. Jane will have told you we got the police. We didn't want to worry your mother. I hope that was right."

"Dead right, Signora."

"Sit down and admire the view. I won't be a moment." She hurried away down the steps on to the path.

I looked at Carl and he looked back at me. "You won't slip away and—"

"I won't do anything to upset anyone," he replied. "Don't worry."

I did worry, knowing his prediliction for taking chances.

Andrew came in, wearing a smile that I thought held genuine warmth. He kissed me on the cheek, shook Carl by the hand. "Lovely to see you both," he said but he did not look at Carl. He looked tense and wary. "We rang the hotel yesterday after Guido came in with the good news that his canoe had been recovered. They said you had gone out."

"We went for a long drive," I said.

"Somewhere interesting?"

"I took Jane into the country."

Andrew sat down. "It's very dry at this time of year. Now tell us about your adventure," he said to Carl. It was clear he was trying but he was not finding this confrontation easy. "How did you get out of the grotto?"

Carl was aware of his difficulty. He set out to charm my father. He was a good storyteller. I sat back with the sun on my closed eyelids listening to his voice.

Chapter Thirteen

We stayed on the terrace for an hour or more drinking the coffee Maria brought us, soaking up the sun. "There will be little enough of it when we get home," Carl said, looking content, not at all like a man who had a furtive job to do.

Donna protested that I must not think of going home yet. I reminded her that a temp had stepped into my job. "If I stay away too long they might decide they like her better than me," I said.

"That would be lovely for us." She reached across and clasped my hand. "Wouldn't it, Andrew?"

"I think you'll find Jane is an independent woman," said my father. "She probably wants to lead her own life."

"Of course." I felt that familiar prickly sensation that came on when Andrew failed to choose his words carefully.

He must have seen something of my reaction in my expression for he added, "She knows she can come back any time she likes."

I smiled at him. We were both trying hard. "Oh yes," said Donna. "So independent you young Englishwomen are these days. Luckily it is not quite the same here." She turned to Carl. "You will stay for lunch, won't you? The children were very upset when they discovered you had gone. Guido wants to thank you."

Carl said we would be delighted. I noted the carefully chosen 'we' and felt it was deliberate. It puzzled me a little. Perhaps he was saying to Donna that it was too late for me to move into the bosom of her family.

"I think I'll go down and bring up Guido's canoe. I'm sure you don't want him to paddle it round to the lido until the sea's calm again."

Donna said, "Really we shouldn't allow you, after all you've done. It's quite heavy."

"I've carried it up," said Andrew. "He's half my age."

He had a way of settling things, I thought, that's his trouble. He's not a flexible man.

"I'm going back to the studio," he said.

Carl rose also, brushed past my chair and surreptitiously pressed the magnifying glass into my hand. "Go with him," he said, or rather breathed, close to my ear.

I jumped up and called after Andrew, "May I come with you?"

He answered without turning round, "I shan't be long. You go with Donna," and disappeared down the steps.

Donna held out her hand, reaching for mine. With my free hand I slipped the magnifying glass into the pocket in my jeans. "Leave him," she said consolingly. "It is not easy for him, having your young man here."

"He's not my young man, Donna," I protested.

"Well, we'll talk. Now, come with me." She led me inside, to the kitchen first to speak to Maria about lunch, then on into the salon. "Let's sit down," she said. When we were side by side on the sofa she began, "Now tell me about Carl. You are in love with him?"

"There's not much point," I said. "You know he's not free."

"You are speaking of Evelina?"

"Who else?"

"I think he loves you."

"I think he loves all women," I said. "He's nice to everyone. I'm a very new friend. And let's face it, Donna, I've been jolly useful to him. Tell me, how did you persuade Andrew not to throw him out?"

She said with a little smile, "I have been trying to convince him that someone will get the story, and that if he cooperates it will be the true one."

I told her about the Italian reporter who came to the hotel and took Carl's story. We laughed about it. "That's what he said. He gave in so the facts would be right. Andrew is going to do the same?"

"I'm not saying I have convinced him. But he was not unwelcoming, was he? It was a shock, Carl's coming."

"Donna, what a diplomat you are!"

She made a little moue of self-deprecation. "So now, let us get back to you. I have something to say. Andrew was not in love with me when I first met him. He still loved your mother and you."

I sat up with a jerk. "*Me*? He hadn't met me."

She ignored my protest, "I made him love me, and that helped him to forget his problems. You and your mother were his problems. You could make this young man fall in love with you. Or is there too much of your father in you?"

I said wryly, "You're seeing the prickly side of me. I'm sorry if I appear resentful. I am. It has been wonderful meeting you and the children. But also, it has shown me how much I've missed. I don't see Andrew as my father. Yet. He deserted me and found a lovely family for himself. It's going to take a while to come to terms with what I've discovered."

She patted my hand. "It is over now. We can't change the past. But you can do what you like with the present."

"Can you, dear Donna? I will certainly try. I'll return. I promise you."

"For Christmas? You will have holidays at Christmas?"

"Yes. Of course. I'd love to come."

"You can afford to? I'm sure Andrew would help."

"Thank you, but no. Now I have a real home to go to from time to time I shall give up my expensive flat which keeps me poor. That's how I compensated," I said wryly. "When my mother died and my stepfather walked away I dealt with the feeling of abandonment by putting down a deposit on a flat that I could make into a nest for myself. Funny things, humans. They need to be safe."

She put an arm round me and hugged me. "I'm so sorry."

Through the open door came a chatter of young voices and the children were all at once flying into the room.

"Jane is back! Jane is back!" That was Lucia.

"And my canoe! My canoe! My canoe!"

Lucia flung herself into my arms and all was bedlam for a while. Maria came running. "*Zitto! Silenzio!*" She was a genius at quietening them.

Lucia shouted at Maria in Italian. These were Italian children, with English as a second language. Donna's admonishing would only be a temporary fix. I saw I was going to have to learn Italian if I were to be close to them. Maria looked to Donna for direction. Donna said, "Yes, she may have lunch with us."

"And sit by Jane?"

"Yes, you may sit by Jane. But only because you asked politely, in English. We all speak English when Jane is here."

I felt a lump at the back of my throat.

Carl appeared in the doorway. Addressed Guido. "I've got your canoe," he said. "Would you like to get the key to the boathouse and help me take it down?"

Guido fled outside shouting, "Come on, come on." Carl grinned and followed him.

"Lunch in fifteen minutes," called Donna after him.

"We'll be back."

It was a jolly lunch. Celebratory, in a way. We were starting to rise from the table when Andrew said casually to Guido, "And were the nuns pleased with the picture?"

"They are going to write you a letter," Guido said. "They've already hung it up."

My heart plummeted. I didn't dare look at Carl.

"Come, children," said Donna, "it's time you were away."

Carl said briskly, "We'll go with them. I'll collect Jane's bag from the hotel and drive her back." The children were delighted. Marisa grasped my hand and pulled me along, up the steps and on to the road. I looked back at Carl who was following with Guido. He gave me the thumbs-up sign.

"So what's good?"

"I thought I might persuade this young man to take us into his school and show us the picture on its new wall."

Guido said, "Yes. I'll show it to you."

I burst out laughing. "How slow of me." I took the magnifying glass out of my pocket and handed it to him. "There you are, ideas man."

"Sister Augustine can speak good English. She'll talk to you," said Guido.

It didn't take long to get to the convent. Perhaps ten minutes. We went up the broad stone steps and waited in an anteroom while Guido searched for Sister Augustine. She came in a flurry of long skirts, a tiny woman with glowing skin, very bright eyes and an enormous butterfly headdress.

"You are Signor Hollis's friends?" Sister Augustine smiled up at us.

"Carl is my friend," said Guido. "He saved my canoe."

"Ah! So you are the hero!" She was delighted to meet him. Her face radiated pleasure. "We have heard a great deal about you this morning, Signor. You spent the night in the cave. We have had two boys who were cut off in that cave. In 1988 it was, I believe. They had their photos in the papers."

I could see we were not going to get away in a hurry. She turned her shining eyes on me. "And you are English? You look English."

Carl expertly diverted her before Guido could butt in with embarrassing explanations of our relationship. "We know you're busy, Sister Augustine. Signor Hollis—"

"They want to see the picture," said Guido.

"Of course. Of course you shall. Follow me."

She led us through a maze of corridors and into a small chapel. "We are very proud of it," Sister Augustine said, standing back with hands folded across her front, gazing up at the *Madonna and Child*. "It is very beautiful."

Carl went close, holding up his magnifying glass.

The nun asked in surprise, "You are looking for a signature? Signor Hollis would not sign it because it is a copy. You must know it's a copy."

"I'm looking at the brush strokes," Carl replied. "I am familiar with the original. I was curious to know how much attention Signor Hollis paid to the brush strokes."

Sister Augustine's amusement disappeared in a flash. She looked at him with great respect. "You are an artist, too?"

"I couldn't paint to this standard," he said.

"How adept you are with words," I said, laughing as we ran down the steps.

"You have to be, in my business. Prevarication and little white lies are part of the trade." He was laughing too.

"So what of Carboni's little bird?"

"Not a sign."

I felt a great surge of triumph.

"Don't get too excited," Carl said. "Andrew did tell you it wasn't one of his best efforts. He may have meant he wasn't paying enough attention to detail. Let's hurry. Time's getting on." He grasped my hand. "Jogging is good for you."

I ran with him. "What's the hurry?"

"I'm going to ring my editor. If he'll wear it, I'm going to get the next flight to Los Angeles."

I was flabbergasted. I stopped dead in the middle of the road. "Why?"

"Come on." He jerked my hand. "Because that's the way you write a story." His excitement was scarcely contained. "The authenticity or otherwise of the picture is the tag line. I want to talk to Grandfather Seizerk now. I need to find the house the picture came from and he's the only one who can tell me."

"How will you locate Grandfather Seizerk? You'll find the art dealer grandson easily enough I imagine, but I'll bet he won't give you any addresses. Hey, you've got to slow down. I'm out of breath."

He settled at a fast walk. "I'm not worth my salt if I can't find the old boy, if he's still alive. There's the catch. Frattuni's grandfather has gone and they'll be much the same age. You see, we've got to find out if the family still exists because they could come forward and claim the picture before it gets to auction. It's only finders keepers if they're not around."

"Oh hell!" I hadn't thought of that. The picture had been stolen in the first place. My thoughts ran back to poor confused Evelina, the dear little baby, and Cesario, who hadn't the money to buy its mother back.

"This is a father of a story, Jane."

I supposed it was. I wondered if he saw the tragedy inherent in it, or if he was thinking solely of his own career. I hadn't read anything he had written. I wondered if his stories touched the heart. Or if they merely exposed matters better hidden. "Do you always work as fast as this?" I asked.

"Always isn't a word that features much in my life." We crossed the piazza where the Duomo stood and headed for the other side of the bay.

"I might go to Amsterdam with my own magnifying glass," I said as we swung up through the narrow streets and headed for the preciptious steps that led to the hotel. "I'm interested in Andrew's reputation."

That caused him to pause. He looked down at me thoughtfully. "Do you know the name of the man he sent the picture to?"

I cast my mind back to the article my friend Rosie had shown me in London. "I don't believe I do. Maybe Andrew would tell me."

"Maybe you won't dare ask him. How do you think he would react to the fact that you were interfering in his affairs?"

"You win again. Do you know his name?"

"Of course."

Yes, of course. What a silly question!

Luigi was in the foyer. "It is a pleasure to have you, Signorina," he said when I explained that I was going. "You will come again?"

"Of course."

"Okay if I ring international, Luigi?" asked Carl.

"*Si, si.* From your room is okay."

I went to my own room and began to pack. Ten minutes later Carl poked his nose in at the door. "I can get away tonight," he said. "I can just about make it to Naples airport if I hurry."

And then he was gone. I went after him. He already had his bag up on the bed and was filling it with a jumble of clothes. "Don't bother to take me to the Villa Passerina," I said. "Andrew will be only too delighted to fetch me."

"Yes, I'm sure he will."

Another man, I couldn't help thinking, might have protested that he could still fulfil his promise if I hurried, but Carl accepted help as he accepted responsibilities. Nothing seemed to dent him.

Except Evelina's treachery.

"Here, let me fold the shirts," I said. "You're making a dog's dinner of them. I'm not much good but I can do a better job than that."

He dropped the shirts on the bed, strode off to the bathroom and came back with his shaving gear. "A cordon bleu dog's dinner it is now," he said, looking down with amusement at my less than professional job. He slammed the lid of the case shut, said, "Right! I'm off," kissed me swiftly on the forehead then picked up his bag and swung away. "I'll call," he said.

I stood there in his empty room feeling abandoned. He hadn't even asked for my London address. After a while I went down and telephoned.

"He was suddenly called away," I told Andrew when he came to pick me up. Andrew didn't comment on or question this astonishing revelation. He merely looked pleased. "So we'll have you all to ourselves."

It was nice of him not to say he was glad to get Carl the newshound off the premises. "For a few more days," I said. "Then I must go back to work."

"Of course."

I felt it was the right answer.

I went back the way I had come, though unaccompanied and paying for my own first class sleeper. Not having had to spend any of those lire I was gloriously in funds.

I stood at the train window looking out on the flat, dry fields of southern Italy. Andrew had said he would send me an air ticket for Christmas. "I haven't done anything for you in all these years," he replied when I protested. "It's the least I can do."

We all knew that between now and Christmas enormous changes would have taken place. The skies might have fallen on him. He might have become a millionaire. I had ventured to ask, "If the painting proves to be a genuine Raphael, would you see Evelina right?"

He looked at me quizzically. "That's a funny thing to say." He repeated it. "See her right? And anyway, it didn't come from her. She was merely the intermediary. The man who owned it, you may remember, was someone called Frattuni. I told you that."

So he had. And I couldn't ask if he would see Frattuni right. I wasn't supposed to know him.

"I was thinking of Evelina's old car," I said, muddling through.

"Are you talking about commission? That's between Frattuni and her," he said in his brisk style. "And by the way, her father gave her a new car. She sold it and kept the money. You may be sure he won't buy her another."

I remembered Cesario saying Evelina sent money when she

could. That she was not unfeeling. I remembered also, because it suited me to, that he had said the child's mother might go back and marry him if he could live in Rome. I wondered if he believed she was, in her own way, in love with him.

The train was slowing down. We were approaching Naples. *Napoli*. I decided I must start adult education classes in Italian, right away.

What was Evelina's game? Did she really think she could continue to live like this, sending money for the child when she could manage it? She must have her head in the sand. Of course her parents would smell a rat sooner or later. And Carl? He was no fool. If she married him he would soon find out she was using his money to provide for her child. Or had she intended to live with him in England, abandoning not only the child but her responsibility to it?

Yet Carl did know. Why was he so silent about it? Was he trying to accustom himself to the idea of accepting the baby? In spite of Signora Frattuni's disinclination to live in the country and care for her, I could not imagine either of them relinquishing the child to another man.

What a mess, I thought, looking out over the rooftops of the jumbled houses on the outskirts of the town. Naples. I thought I might get a cup of coffee here.

Roma. Bologna. Milano. Night fell outside. The moon shone down as the train rushed helter-skelter in and out of tunnels. Only a small slice had been taken off it since it had been round enough and bright enough to light my way down to the grotto when Carl was imprisoned in the cave. It showed me a little of the mountains as the train sped through.

Where was Carl now? Battling with a suspicious young Seizerk for his grandfather's telephone number? Flying back clutching the address of some German stately home gone to ruin? Rebuilt perhaps by the family who would come forward when Carl's story was published, claiming the picture was theirs? Would Carl tell them? Or would he stand aside and wait for them to find out? Would that be his next story?

We headed into the darkness of another tunnel. Pounded out again. Yes, I could see the mountains in the moonlight, vast white rocks they were. The towering Dolomites?

Would Carl, in writing his story, clear Andrew's name? Would Andrew overcome his bitterness and face the world?

I wished I could roll all my problems – no, not mine, other people's – into a bundle and lock them in my suitcase. I had no problems except of the heart. Time heals. Would my heart heal?

The train was slowing. Another station? I stared up at the mountain opposite, black-shadowed and grand.

I didn't want to be healed. I wanted to see Carl again and hear him say he'd sorted Evelina out. Sent her to Frattuni where she belonged. I wouldn't at all mind taking up the broken threads of his life. I could bear to wait for time to mend them. What was it Donna had said about making a man love you? I felt devoid of pride in my new aloneness. When one has tasted such excitement, one is more than ever alone.

For heaven's sake, I said to myself, get out of your clothes and lie down and go to sleep. I got into the narrow bed. The drumming of the wheels, the roar of the tunnels, that was my night.

"Good lord!" shrieked Rosie down the telephone, "you're back! How did you get on? What happened?"

"If you're not going to one of your exhibitions tonight I'll feed you," I said, "and I'll tell you how I got on. If you are, I'd like to go with you. I'm suddenly into art." A little white lie; a prevarication, Carl had called this sort of thing. I wanted to talk to people. Hear what they had to say about the *Madonna and Child* that the disgraced Andrew Hollis had sent to Amsterdam.

"No luck for tonight," said Rosie, "but I'd be delighted if you'd feed me." She could always be prevailed upon to come to supper. You did not work on her kind of magazine for the money. Besides, she could have gone into debt buying me that lunch at the Groucho. My thoughts stilled. She hadn't paid for the lunch. Or the gin. The bill would have gone to Carl's employers.

She arrived from work at six o'clock wearing a beret with a pompom, a tiny miniskirt, high heels and black stockings. An unlit cigarette wobbled between her fingers.

"This is a no smoking zone," I said sternly. "Put it away if you please."

She dropped it casually into her handbag. "It's my new

trademark. I've taken to appearing in doorways with this ciggy. It's getting worn out. One needs a trademark if one isn't to disappear among the extraverts I swill around with." She flung her enormous bag down on the floor.

"You're good for me," I said. "I haven't been laughing very much in the last few days."

"Was it as bad as that? Now tell me, do tell me—"

I cut her off. "You put Carl Beaumont on to me."

"Of course." She took off the preposterous beret, flung it on the coffee table and dropped onto the sofa. "Isn't he dreamy? Did you fall in love?"

I said, carefully keeping the bitterness out of my voice, "He'd kiss anyone for a story."

"Is that all that happened? I thought he was dead right for you. I thought you'd at least come home engaged."

"You did it for him," I accused her, "so he could write about my father."

"Don't look so cross. I did it for both of you. Life's a pig," said Rosie, "but you can make it a lot better if you help one another. Such luxury you have here." She fingered the upholstery. "Compared to my bedsit this is Buckingham Palace."

"Enjoy it while you can," I said. "It's up for grabs. I don't need it any more. I need money for air fares."

"I'm so glad." She looked at me kindly. "I thought there was something very sad about your living alone in this 'real home' all by yourself."

I cooked an Italian meal, veal in Marsala sauce except that I hadn't had time to buy the Marsala so made do with sherry. We talked and wept and talked again. Rosie wept easily with me. Tears of emotion, happiness mingled with despair. We drank quite a lot of the Amoretta Andrew had pressed on me and got a little tight. It was a blood-letting. Somebody had said, in Italy, 'What it is to have friends.' I tried to remember who.

It was nearly two weeks later that Andrew rang with the great news that the *Madonna and Child* had been pronounced an authentic Raphael. "One of those paintings that disappeared centuries ago," he said. "It's going to be auctioned at Sothebys."

"How wonderful! How absolutely wonderful! Will you come for the auction and stay with me?"

"It isn't my picture, you know."

But it was. It was so very much his picture. That Madonna held his reputation in her sweet smile.

"And you're selling your flat."

"Not yet. I won't, now, until after the auction."

"These things take time," he said. "It will be a month or so. They have to get it in the catalogue."

"Of course. But you must come." I saw his coming to London, talking to the art world, as part of his therapy.

"I'll consult with Donna."

I smiled down the telephone knowing what Donna would say.

And then Carl came. I opened the door and there he was. I said the first silly thing that came into my head. "I didn't know you had my address."

"That's not a welcome." He kissed me on the mouth, slowly, generously, as though now he had all the time in the world to spare. I was dizzy with shock. I backed into the room. He followed me and stood looking round at the shelves of paperbacks; the pile of newly-acquired Ben Tyrill art books; the decent furniture, second-hand, but carefully chosen. "This is quite a pad," he said.

"You can buy it if you like. It's going after the family have been to stay." It struck me how easily 'the family' had slid off my tongue, with pride.

"I just might," said this past master at pleasing people. "Yes, why not? But you don't want to leave." He looked at me. A long, thoughtful look, into my emotions and halfway to my heart.

"It's my home," I said. "I needed it badly when I bought it and it has served me well. Now I've a family home to go to, I don't need it any more."

"Don't you?" He went on looking at me, quizzical now.

"I can't afford it as well as frequent trips to Amalfi. That's really what I mean."

He thrust his hands down in his pockets, examined the windows, the ceiling, the fourth-hand, professionally mended

Turkish carpet. He seemed to be taking my home into his mind.

"You haven't thought this out," he said. "You can't go back. An independent woman can't metamorphose into a daughter in a bedsit, living for visits to the family."

I felt taken over.

"There's a lot to talk about," he said. "I've booked a table for dinner. Get your things on."

I heard him moving round the flat, looking at things. Opening doors. I wondered whether reporters did this all the time, or if he really did want to buy my flat. When I emerged dressed in a pink two piece and high heels, ready to hold my own in the kind of smart restaurant I assumed we were going to, he took my hand and kissed it. "What a beauty! As Donna said, 'Why do they have to live in jeans, these English girls?'" And without waiting for an answer, "Come on. We'll pick up a taxi."

"Aren't you going to tell me what happened?" I asked as he took the keys from me and locked the door.

"Sure." He hustled me down the stairs.

"So nothing much happened, in the end?"

"Oh yes. A great deal. But you don't talk about a story before it's written."

"I won't tell anyone."

"It's not that. Talking weakens it. It gets into the air and gets lost."

I took my time digesting that. "Tell me one thing," I ventured. "Are you going to demolish my father's reputation?"

"You know he hasn't got one," Carl said. "I hope my story will help to reinstate the one he had."

He hailed a taxi and bundled me in. "I'll tell you all you need to know," he said as we settled down together in the back seat. "Old Seizerk was a mine of information. His grandson is being sued by the Bolivian millionaire who intends to come over and bid for the *Madonna* at Sothebys. He's determined to have it. Multi, he is. You can have anything if you're a multi-millionaire," said Carl. "The house it came from was razed to the ground by the Allied bombing which makes a hero out of the late grandfather Frattuni for saving the *Madonna* for posterity. The owners were exterminated at Auschwitz.

Evelina's going to marry Frattuni. Your father's taking a commission – at Donna's insistence."

"Donna!"

"She's an exceptional woman, your stepmother. She can speak up when she wants to. Taking a commission gets him involved. D'you see?"

We stopped at the traffic lights. He took my hand. "Now that's enough of other people. This is your time. Yours and mine."

"I'm glad," I said, trying to be witty and sophisticated, but sounding emotional. "I do seem to inhabit a spot right at the bottom of your list of priorities."

"There's a better way of putting it. The best part of a story is its ending."

The taxi stopped. My brain was spinning. He helped me out and paid the driver. I went into the restaurant in a daze. The chandeliers were blazing. There were smiling people everywhere. Smiling at us as people do when they see a happy woman dressed to kill, accompanied by a handsome man. The head waiter was delighted to see us. He led us to our table with a flourish.

Carl ordered champagne. I waited for what was going to happen, now that Carl had time. I heard him say, "You will understand I had to clear the decks, first."

"Yes."

"And wait for you to get the Italian thing in perspective."

"Yes."

"I'll buy your flat, but only if you will stay."

"Oh yes."

He held my hands across the table. I looked into those dark velvet Mediterranean eyes and stopped breathing.

"Italian parents don't like their children shacking up together. We half Italians are very obedient to our parents. Very family oriented. Wait for it. I'm about to propose."

"I'm waiting," I managed, holding the answer ready on the end of my tongue.

He was right about the most important part of any story being its ending.

Dead right.